NICOLE CLARKSTON

THE DEBUTANTE and the SPY

Rogues in Disguise Book Three

PROPER ROMANCE

Cover Design by GetCovers.com
Cover Image Licensed by Period Images
Background image licensed by Shutterstock

Blog and Website: https://nicoleclarkston.com/
Newsletter: subscribepage.io/V5dPFd
Book Bub: https://www.bookbub.com/profile/nicole-clarkston
Facebook: https://www.facebook.com/NicoleClarkstonAuthor
Twitter: https://twitter.com/N_Clarkston
Amazon: https://www.amazon.com/Nicole-Clarkston
Austen Variations: http://austenvariations.com/

Contents

Chapter One

THE DAWN MIST CLUNG to the forest like a shroud, heavy and damp, muffling the sounds of distant musket fire. Robert Daniels moved through the underbrush, his breath steady and controlled, each exhale a cloud of vapour in the cold morning air. The fog reduced the world around him to a murky palette of greys and greens, but his eyes were sharp, his senses alert. Every step was deliberate, his feet moving silently over the damp leaves and tangled roots beneath.

Robert's broad shoulders strained against his rough, plain clothing, the fabric stretched tight across the muscles that had been forged at his father's anvil long before he took up a rifle for the Crown. His calloused hands gripped a flintlock pistol, its weight familiar and reassuring. He'd grown used to carrying a weapon, even if he still felt more at home with a hammer. But today, it wasn't a hammer that would save Pierre Lavoisier's life.

Pierre, his informant—a French civilian who had risked everything to pass intelligence to the British—was in danger. Robert had planned to meet him in a small clearing, a discreet exchange for the kind of information that saved lives. But something had gone wrong. The British patrol had found Pierre first, and now Robert could hear the mocking laughter of soldiers ahead, mingled with Pierre's desperate pleas. He had to move fast, but he also had to be smart.

Musket fire cracked in the distance. Robert's heart hammered in his chest, but he kept his pace measured. He couldn't afford to be seen. If the British soldiers spotted him now, dressed in plain clothes, they wouldn't hesitate to shoot him as a spy—or worse, they might recognise him. The thought sent a shiver down his spine, colder than the morning mist. He was dressed like a French peasant, deep in British territory, and the 'enemy' wore the same uniform he once had.

As he neared the clearing, Robert dropped to a crouch, moving slowly now, using the thick underbrush as cover. He could see them up ahead—two British soldiers, their muskets pointed at Pierre, who was tied to a tree. The younger of the two soldiers, a sergeant, was taunting Pierre, waving his musket in the air.

"French blighter," the sergeant sneered, his voice laced with contempt. "Think you can play both sides and get away with it? Traitor's a traitor, no matter whose side he's on."

Robert's grip tightened on his pistol. He couldn't take them head-on. A direct confrontation would draw the attention of every British patrol in the area. Fifty soldiers would be on him in minutes, and that was if the French didn't find him first. No, he had to be quiet. Precise. He had to get Pierre out without spilling any British blood—not just for Pierre's sake, but for his own mission. If the British suspected him of betrayal, his entire assignment would be compromised.

He inched closer, his movements slow and deliberate, keeping low to the ground. Every muscle in his body was tense, ready to spring into action. His mind raced through the possibilities. He could try to distract them, draw them away from Pierre. But how? He didn't have time to think. The sergeant was raising his musket, aiming it at Pierre's chest.

Robert's heart pounded in his ears. He had to act. *Now.*

Taking a deep breath, he crept around to the side, his body pressed close to the ground. He spotted a rock nearby, picked it up, and hurled it into the bushes on the opposite side of the clearing. The soldiers' heads whipped around at the sudden noise, their muskets following their gaze. In that split second, Robert lunged forward, crossing the distance to Pierre in two long strides.

"Quiet," he whispered, his voice low and steady as he cut through the ropes binding Pierre to the tree. Pierre's eyes widened in surprise, but he didn't make a sound.

The soldiers turned back just as Robert grabbed Pierre by the arm, pulling him into the cover of the trees. One of them shouted, raising his musket. Robert didn't wait to see if he would fire. He dragged Pierre deeper into the woods, his large frame moving quickly despite the branches that snagged at his clothes and the underbrush that clawed at his legs.

They were almost clear when a musket ball whizzed past his ear, thudding into the trunk of a tree beside him. Another shot rang out, this one grazing his shoulder. He grunted in pain but kept moving. If they got caught, it was all over.

"Keep moving," he hissed to Pierre, pushing him ahead. The Frenchman stumbled, his legs weak from hours of captivity, but Robert's iron grip kept him upright. The pain in his shoulder flared with every step, but he pushed it aside. He'd survived worse. He could survive this.

Musket fire erupted from the treeline again. The French had joined the fray, firing blindly into the fog in reply to the British volley. They needed a plan—a way out. He couldn't afford to be seen by the British, but he also couldn't let the French soldiers take them. They would be just as ruthless, if not more so.

"There's a ravine up ahead," Robert said, his voice low but urgent. "We can use it for cover."

Pierre nodded, his breath coming in ragged gasps. Robert led them toward the ravine, keeping low, moving as quickly as he could without drawing attention. He could feel the blood running down his arm, the pain sharp and insistent, but he didn't slow. They reached the edge of the ravine, and Robert jumped down first, his boots hitting the soft earth with a dull thud. He turned and caught Pierre as he leapt down after him, nearly lifting him off the ground with one hand.

"We need to get to the farmhouse," Robert said, his voice tight with pain. "It's not far. We can hide there until nightfall."

Pierre nodded again, too winded to speak. They moved along the ravine, the sound of gunfire growing fainter behind them. Robert's mind was a whirl of thoughts—what would he do once they reached the farmhouse? He couldn't stay here. The mission was too important. He needed the information Pierre had, the reason he had come this far into enemy territory in the first place.

When they reached the farmhouse, Robert pushed open the door with his good shoulder, glancing around. It was empty, abandoned. Good. They had a little time to breathe. He turned to Pierre, who was slumped against the wall, his face pale.

"Are you hurt?" Robert asked, his voice softer now.

Pierre shook his head. "No... just... tired. Thank you, monsieur. You saved my life."

Robert nodded, setting his pistol on the table. "We're not out of this yet," he said, though there was a hint of relief in his voice. "I need to know, Pierre—what did you find? What was so important that you risked coming back here?"

Pierre took a deep breath, still trying to steady himself. "It's worse than I told you before. There's a man in London—high up, someone with influence. He's been passing information to the French, feeding them our plans. I heard his name... Aston. I think he's called Lord Aston."

Robert felt his heart drop into his stomach. *Lord Aston.* Carmella's father. He'd heard whispers about the man before, but nothing concrete. If what Pierre was saying was true, it meant someone close to Carmella—someone Robert once admired—was a traitor to the Crown.

"Are you certain?" Robert asked.

Pierre nodded. "As certain as I can be. I overheard two French officers. One of them mentioned something... something about a plan to disrupt funding for the navy from within."

Robert paced the confines of the farmhouse, his fingers drumming nervously in the air as he thought through the possibilities. He had to get back to England, had to find out if this was true. If Lord Aston was indeed a traitor, it could mean disaster for the British war effort. And it could mean that Carmella was in danger, too.

"We need to move," he said, his voice steady. "I have to get this information to my superiors. And you... you need to get somewhere safe."

Pierre nodded, his eyes filled with gratitude and fear. Robert glanced out the window, scanning the treeline for any sign of movement. The forest was quiet, but he knew better than to trust that silence. They were running out of time.

"We go now," Robert said, grabbing his pistol and reloading it with a swift, practised motion. "Stay close. And whatever you do, don't stop running."

As they slipped out of the farmhouse and back into the woods, Robert felt a familiar resolve settle over him. He had a name now and some idea of where to start looking. And if it were true, if Lord Aston was a traitor, Robert would do whatever it took to protect Carmella from the fallout.

Even if it meant facing the demons of his past and risking everything he had fought so hard to build.

"Lady Carmella, you seem quite alone this evening." Roland Hawthorne's voice broke through the low hum of conversation around her. Carmella startled, dropping her lace fan. Roland bent to retrieve it, his movements graceful, practised, every inch the perfect gentleman. He rose and extended the fan toward her with a slight bow, his eyes never leaving her face.

"Thank you, Mr Hawthorne," Carmella replied, taking the fan with a forced smile. She tried to calm the unease fluttering in her chest. "I was merely enjoying a moment to myself."

Roland's smile widened, but there was something predatory in his gaze, something that set her on edge. "A moment alone, at such a grand ball? Surely, that cannot be as enjoyable as having some agreeable company," he said smoothly, stepping closer. "I had hoped you would grant me the honour of a dance."

Carmella hesitated, glancing around the crowded ballroom. Everywhere she looked, there were familiar faces—friends, acquaintances, even a few rivals—all watching, judging. The very idea of dancing with Roland filled her with a sense of dread. His touch, though never improper, always felt possessive, as if he believed she was already his. She knew he wanted to press his suit, to secure her hand in marriage, and her father had all but given his blessing. But the thought of such a future made her stomach turn.

"Perhaps later," she said, keeping her tone light, polite. "I find myself a bit weary this evening."

Roland's expression flickered, just for a moment, before he regained his composure. "Weary? At such a lively gathering?" he asked, his voice soft, coaxing. "You are far too young and beautiful to be weary, Miss Neville. Perhaps what you need is a change of scenery. A stroll on the terrace, perhaps?"

Carmella stiffened, her smile faltering. "The ballroom is quite sufficient, I assure you."

"Of course," Roland replied. His tone was respectful, but his eyes betrayed his frustration. He leaned closer, lowering his voice. "I spoke with your father earlier. He seems quite eager for us to settle matters, to make our arrangement official."

Her heart sank at his words. She had feared as much, had seen the way her father and Roland spoke in hushed tones, exchanging knowing looks. Lord Aston had been growing more insistent, more anxious for her to accept Roland's proposal, to secure a match that would benefit their family. And yet, everything in her rebelled at the thought.

"I... I have not yet made a decision," she said carefully, trying to keep her voice steady.

"Your hesitation is understandable, of course," Roland said, though his grip on her arm tightened slightly. "Naturally, we desire to consult your wishes in this as well. But you must know that your father and I both have your best interests at heart."

The words felt like a noose tightening around her throat. She forced a smile, pulling her arm gently from his grasp. "I appreciate your concern, Mr Hawthorne, truly. But I must ask for more time to consider."

He inclined his head, though his smile did not reach his eyes. "As you wish. But do not keep me waiting too long, my dear. A man can only be patient for so long."

Carmella nodded, her heart pounding. She watched as Roland moved away, disappearing into the crowd. The moment he was gone, she sighed loudly enough to be overheard from several paces away.

But no one was there to hear her.

No one was there, because they were all talking, laughing, dancing... not a soul would even notice if she just slipped away this moment. She felt trapped, suffocated, as though the walls of the ballroom were closing in around her. She needed air. Desperately.

She turned and made her way toward the open doors that led to the terrace, weaving through the guests with as much grace as she could muster. The cool night air was a welcome relief, washing over her heated skin as she stepped outside. She closed her eyes, inhaling deeply, trying to calm her racing heart.

"Carmella."

Her eyes snapped open at the sound of her father's voice. She turned to see Lord Aston standing in the shadows near the edge of the terrace, his face partially obscured. "Father," she said, surprised. "I did not see you there."

Lord Aston stepped forward, his expression tense, his eyes darting around as if to ensure no one else was near. "What are you doing out here?" he asked, his voice low, almost a whisper. "You should be inside, mingling with the guests."

"I needed a moment," she said softly. "The ballroom is rather stifling tonight."

Her father's eyes narrowed slightly. "I saw you speaking with Mr Hawthorne. Have you given him an answer?"

Carmella swallowed, her unease growing. "I... I have not yet decided."

Lord Aston's expression darkened. "You must not delay, Carmella. Mr Hawthorne is a good match. You would do well to accept his suit."

A flicker of defiance sparked within her. "And if I do not wish to marry Mr Hawthorne?"

Her father's gaze hardened. "You will do as you are told. Our family's future depends on it."

The coldness in his voice sent a shiver down her spine. She had always known her father to be a man of duty, propriety—he would never be the man to choose sentiment over what was expected of him. But there was something different about him now, something darker. She had noticed it over the past few weeks—the late-night meetings, the hushed conversations, the way he seemed to be constantly looking over his shoulder. She wondered what could be troubling him so, but she knew better than to ask directly.

"I understand," she said quietly, lowering her gaze. "But I must have more time to... accustom myself to the idea."

Lord Aston nodded curtly. "Very well. But do not delay too long. Time is not a luxury we have."

With that, he turned and walked back into the ballroom, leaving Carmella standing alone on the terrace, her mind spinning. What did he mean by that? What was happening that made time so precious? Her father was always involved in some sort of business dealings, but this felt different—more urgent, more dangerous.

She turned to look out over the city, the lights of London twinkling like stars against the darkened sky. She had always loved this view, had always found comfort in the steady, unchanging beauty of it. But tonight, even the familiar sight of the city felt foreign, distant. She felt a sense of unease, a feeling that something was terribly wrong.

As she stood there, lost in thought, she heard a rustle behind her. She turned quickly, half expecting to see Roland or her father, but instead, she saw a figure slipping out from the shadows—a man, tall and broad-shouldered, his face partially hidden by the brim of his hat.

For a moment, her heart leapt into her throat. *Could it be?* No, it was impossible. Robert was gone. He had been gone for years. And yet, as the man stepped into the light, she saw the familiar set of his shoulders, the way he moved with that same quiet grace she remembered.

"Robert?" she whispered, her voice shaking.

The man paused, his head turning slightly toward her. For a brief moment, their eyes met, and she felt a jolt of recognition, a spark of something she had thought long extinguished. But then, just as quickly, he turned and disappeared into the shadows, leaving her standing there, her heart pounding in her chest.

Had it really been him? Or was her mind playing tricks on her, conjuring ghosts from her past to haunt her? She didn't know. All she knew was that the sight of him—real or imagined—had stirred something deep within her, something she had tried so hard to bury.

She needed to know. She needed answers. About her father, about Robert, about everything. She couldn't continue living like this, caught between duty and desire, between fear and hope. Couldn't keep loving a ghost.

Chapter Two

"Captain," Robert greeted, sliding into the booth across from Nicholas Hunt. The pub was dimly lit, the smell of ale and smoke heavy in the air. He kept his voice low, his eyes darting around to make sure no one was paying them undue attention. "I appreciate you meeting me on such short notice."

"It's just Hunt, now, Daniels. I've been out of uniform for over a year now."

"Old habits, sir," he grinned.

Hunt gave a curt nod, his gaze steady. "I wasn't expecting to see you back in London so soon. Thought France had its claws in you for a while longer."

Robert's mouth twitched in a semblance of a smile. "France's troubles follow me wherever I go, it seems." He leaned forward, his tone dropping to a near whisper. "I've come across something troubling."

Hunt's expression shifted, his brows knitting together. "Go on."

"There's a man," Robert began, keeping his voice level, "a man of influence. Aristocratic. He's well connected in London society, and from what I've gathered, he may be working for the French."

"He would not be the only one," Hunt grunted, but then he paused, his eyes narrowed slightly. "You've got more than a hunch, I take it?"

Robert nodded, his face grim. "I came across intelligence in France from a contact who had risked his life to provide it. The kind of information that could have only come from someone with direct access to high-level discussions—naval plans, ship movements, funding bills being deliberately tampered with. Someone in London is feeding this to the enemy, and it's not just idle talk. There's substance."

Hunt took a slow sip of his drink, then set the tankard down with deliberate care. "And you think this man—this aristocrat—is your source?"

"Too many pieces fit," Robert replied. "He's in the right circles, attends the right parties, has the ear of the right people. He's always been a bit of a mystery, but lately, there have been more whispers, more signs. His name came up in connection with some of the leaks we've been tracking."

Hunt leaned back, folding his arms. "If this is true, it's a jolly sight worse than we thought. You're suggesting a member of the peerage could be a traitor to the Crown?"

Robert's jaw tightened. "I don't want to believe it, but the evidence is mounting. I've already confirmed that he is in London. He was just at Lady Hargrave's ball last night. I know where to find him, how to follow him."

Hunt nodded slowly, his face pensive. "You said he's got access to military plans. How high up does this go? Are we talking operational details or something more sensitive?"

"More sensitive," Robert said, his tone grave. "If what I've been told is accurate, he's got information on strategic decisions—plans that could alter the course of the war if they fall into the wrong hands. And he's not just passing on scraps; he's giving the French a full picture."

Hunt's eyes flicked to Robert's, searching. "Why would he do it? Money? Influence?"

"Could be either. Could be something else entirely," Robert replied. "But from what I've seen, it's not just about greed. There's something else driving him—desperation, maybe. Or leverage. I've seen the type before."

Hunt considered this, then leaned forward. "And you're sure he's the one?"

Robert hesitated. "No. That's why I need to get closer. I need to confirm it before we move. If we act too soon, he'll go underground or change tactics. And if we act too late, the damage could be irreversible."

A silence fell between them as the former commanding officer's eyes grew hazy in thought. Finally, Hunt spoke. "And what's your plan, then? Just going to waltz into his drawing room and ask him outright?"

Robert gave a small, humourless laugh. "Not quite. I need to observe him, follow his movements. Get a sense of who he talks to, what he does. I need to be in the right places at the right times without tipping him off."

Hunt nodded. "You said you saw him at Lady Hargrave's ball?"

"Yes," Robert confirmed. "I stayed out of sight, but I saw enough to know he's hiding something. His movements were too deliberate, his conversations too quiet. He's planning something, and I need to find out what."

"Then you're going to need more than just eyes and ears," Hunt said. "You're going to need a way in, someone who can vouch for you, give you an excuse to be where you need to be."

"I was hoping you might have some ideas."

Hunt rubbed his chin thoughtfully. "There's a garden party at the Bexleys' estate in a few days. The kind of event where the high and mighty feel secure, relaxed. If he's planning something, he might let his guard down there."

Robert hesitated. "I cannot be seen, sir."

"Poppycock. It is not as if you will march in there wearing a uniform. We will be sure you look the part."

"It is not that. My face, I..."

Hunt tilted his head. "You're afraid someone will recognise you?"

Robert held his breath, then let it out with a slow nod. "Beyond any doubt. A garden party, sir..."

"Then we dress you as a gardener," Hunt said with a casual wave of his hand. "Those rich blokes don't even look at the gardeners."

Robert swallowed. Carmella would *certainly* notice him dressed as a gardener. "I think, sir, that would be even worse."

"Hang it all, Daniels, do you want my help, or do you not? I can get you into this garden party, but not if you turn into a milksop quaking in your boots!" He frowned, his gray eyes piercing. "Who is this person? Someone who could expose you?"

"I do not..." Robert's brow furrowed, and he shook his head. "No, not... not in that sense."

"Then we've nothing to worry about. Carry on as if you've all the right in the world to be there, and do not borrow trouble."

Robert nodded. "Yes, sir, but that is just it. I'll need a reason to be there. A way to blend in."

"I can arrange that," Hunt said, his eyes narrowing in thought. "An old friend from the army, back in town, looking to make a few connections. It's vague enough to be plausible, and you won't stand out too much. But you'll need to play the part—be charming, but not too forward."

Robert allowed a hint of a smile. "You're giving me advice on charm, Captain?"

Hunt chuckled, a rare sound from him. "Don't let it go to your head, Daniels. Just remember, these people are sharp. One wrong move, and they'll sniff you out like a fox in a henhouse. You'll have to mind your city manners."

"I understand. I won't make any mistakes."

A pause stretched between them, and then Hunt leaned forward, his voice dropping even lower. "One more thing, Daniels. You've been in this game long enough to know that when someone starts feeding information to the enemy, they're not working alone. If this man is our mole, there could be others—inside and outside London."

Robert nodded. "I've thought of that. It's why I've been cautious. I can't risk tipping my hand too early."

"Good," Hunt said. "Keep it that way. And watch your back. If he's working with others, they'll be watching you too."

"Right." Robert leaned back, studying Hunt for a moment. "How's domestic life treating you, Captain? Not missing the field too much, I hope."

Hunt gave a small, wry smile. "The roads and bivouacks are bleeding simpler than dealing with my family, I'll tell you that much. They think I'm wasting my talents by not taking a seat in Parliament. Can you imagine me as a politician?"

Robert chuckled. "You'd scare half of them out of their wits. Which might not be a bad thing, come to think of it."

"Maybe," Hunt agreed, his smile fading. "But I'll take an evening with Bess over French sabres any day. And you, Daniels? Any thoughts of settling down?"

Robert's face darkened slightly. "I had thoughts," he said quietly. "Once. But those days are behind me now."

Hunt watched him carefully. "You've still got time. The war won't last forever."

Robert shrugged. "Maybe. But right now, there's work to be done. I can't afford distractions."

"Fair enough," Hunt said, finishing his drink. "Just don't let it eat away at you. This line of work... it's not for the faint of heart."

"I know," Robert replied. "And I've made my peace with it."

Hunt nodded. "All right, then. We've got our plan. I'll see you at the Bexleys'."

Robert stood, giving a slight nod. "Thank you, Captain. I appreciate the help."

Hunt waved a hand dismissively. "Just be careful, Daniels. Remember, the higher up you go, the harder the fall."

Robert turned to leave, but something in Hunt's tone made him pause. "What is it, Captain?"

Hunt hesitated, then said, "Just... keep your eyes open. And remember, in this city, no one is who they seem."

Robert nodded, a grim smile touching his lips. "Don't worry, Captain. I've learned that lesson well enough."

"Lady Carmella, your father was quite particular about your swift return," Mrs Dunn reminded her as they stepped out of the carriage. The late afternoon sun cast a warm glow across the cobbled street, but the unease in Carmella's chest felt cold and heavy.

"Yes, Mrs Dunn, I am aware," Carmella replied, keeping her tone polite as they ascended the steps to the townhouse. This morning's call on Lady Beauchamp had been nothing more than a distraction, a way to delay the inevitable conversation with her father. She could feel the tension building, like a storm gathering on the horizon.

The butler opened the door before they reached it. "Welcome home, Lady Carmella, Mrs Dunn," he said with a respectful nod. "Lord Aston requests your presence in his study, immediately."

Carmella inclined her head, her heart tightening. "Thank you, Whitmore. I shall attend him at once." She handed her gloves to Mrs Dunn, who gave her a small, encouraging smile.

"Do not keep him waiting, my lady."

Carmella nodded, then squared her shoulders and made her way down the hallway. The familiar walls seemed to close in around her, their heavy tapestries suffocating. She paused outside her father's study, drew in a deep breath, and knocked softly.

"Enter," came the clipped voice from within.

She pushed open the door and stepped inside, keeping her posture straight and her expression neutral. The study was dimly lit, and her father sat behind his large desk, a pile of documents spread before him. His gaze was sharp as it lifted to meet hers, and she could see the lines of worry etched into his face.

"You wished to see me, Father?" Carmella asked, closing the door gently behind her.

Lord Aston did not immediately respond. He set down the letter he had been reading and gestured to the chair opposite his desk. "Sit down, Carmella," he said, his tone measured but firm.

She obeyed, smoothing her skirts as she took her seat. She could feel his eyes on her, weighing her, judging her. She had been prepared for this, but it did not make the moment any easier.

"I understand you were in the ladies' retiring room for the rest of the evening last night," he began, his laced with a hint of displeasure. "Care to explain why?"

Carmella hesitated, choosing her words carefully. "I was feeling unwell, Father. The ballroom was quite warm, and I thought it best to retire."

"Unwell?" he repeated, his tone sceptical. "Or was it merely an excuse to avoid Mr Hawthorne's attentions?"

Carmella felt a flush rise to her cheeks. "I assure you, Father, I was genuinely—"

"Enough," he interrupted, holding up a hand. "I have spoken with Mr Hawthorne. He is a good man, and he has expressed a sincere interest in you. This reluctance of yours is unbecoming."

She looked down at her hands, her fingers twisting in her lap. "I am not certain Mr Hawthorne and I are well suited. I need more time to consider."

"Time?" Lord Aston's voice sharpened. "Time is a luxury we do not have, Carmella. You are of age, and it is your duty to secure a match that benefits this family. Mr Hawthorne is wealthy, respectable, and willing. What more could you possibly want?"

"Perhaps a choice," she said before she could stop herself.

Her father's eyes narrowed. "A choice? You speak as if this is some frivolous matter. Do you think your mother had a choice? Do you think any of us have choices in matters of duty and honour?"

Carmella's throat tightened, the words caught there. "I only wish to be happy, Father."

"And you think a choice will guarantee that?" he scoffed, leaning back in his chair. "Happiness is fleeting, Carmella. A strong marriage, a good match—that is what endures. You will learn this in time."

She wanted to argue, to protest, but she knew it would do no good. Her father was not a man easily swayed, especially when he believed he was acting in the best interest of the family.

"There is more at stake here than your whims," he continued, his tone softening slightly, though his expression remained stern. "I have worked hard to ensure our standing in society. The right marriage is crucial. Mr Hawthorne is... ideal."

She swallowed hard, feeling the sting of tears but refusing to let them fall. "And if I cannot bring myself to accept him?"

Her father's face hardened again. "Then you would do well to learn to accept what is best for you. You are a woman of rank, Lady Carmella. You do not have the luxury of indulging every fancy or desire."

A tense silence settled between them, and Carmella could feel the weight of his words pressing down on her like a physical force. She had known this conversation was coming, had dreaded it for days, but still, it felt like a punch to the stomach.

"I saw you looking at that man last night," Lord Aston said suddenly, his tone sharper. "You seemed... distant."

Carmella's heart skipped a beat. "Who?"

"The man in the shadows," her father replied, his eyes narrowing. "Near the terrace. You looked at him as if you had seen a ghost. Who was he?"

She blinked, taken aback. For a moment, she thought she had imagined seeing Robert at the ball, thought her mind had played tricks on her, conjuring ghosts from the past. But her father had seen him, too.

"I... I don't know," she stammered, her voice unsteady. "It was dark. I couldn't see clearly."

Lord Aston leaned forward, his gaze piercing. "You are lying to me, Carmella."

"I swear, Father, I do not know who he was," she insisted, the panic rising in her chest. "He disappeared before I could see his face."

He studied her for a long moment, his eyes cold, calculating. "I do not appreciate deception, Carmella. Nor do I tolerate disobedience. Whoever he was, I want you to stay away from him. Do you understand?"

"Yes, Father," she whispered, her heart pounding. "I understand."

Another silence, thicker, more oppressive. Then Lord Aston leaned back, his expression softening ever so slightly. "I do not wish to be harsh with you, Carmella," he said quietly. "But you must see reason. This is not a game. Our family's future is at stake."

She nodded, though her mind was already spinning, her thoughts racing back to the shadowed figure she had glimpsed at the ball. Could it have been Robert? Had he truly returned? And if so, why now?

"Is there anything else, Father?" she asked, her voice trembling slightly.

"No," he said after a moment. "That will be all. But remember what I have said. This frivolity must end. You must decide—and soon."

She stood, her legs feeling shaky beneath her. "I will consider your words carefully, Father," she said, keeping her tone neutral. "May I be excused?"

He nodded, waving a dismissive hand. "Go. And remember, Carmella—your duty comes before your desires."

She turned and left the study, her heart heavy, her mind racing. She needed answers. She needed to know who that man was, why he had been at the ball, and what he wanted. She could not afford to wait any longer. She needed to act.

As she moved down the hallway, she heard a quiet knock at the front door. She paused, curiosity prickling at her. The butler opened the door to reveal a man dressed in a heavy cloak, his face partially hidden. He spoke in hushed tones, asking to see Lord Aston, insisting it was a matter of urgency.

Carmella stayed hidden in the shadows, watching as her father emerged from his study and greeted the visitor. The look on her father's face was tense, almost fearful, as he ushered the man into the study and closed the door behind them.

Her heart began to race. Who was this man? And what could be so urgent that he would come at such a late hour? She felt a chill run down her spine, her suspicions growing. She had to find out more.

Her father's guarded behaviour and the mysterious visitor had only deepened her curiosity. Something had changed in the last few months, and it seemed to concern her… or rather, her marriage prospects. But confronting him directly was out of the question—he would dismiss her concerns, or worse, become angry. No, she needed to be more discreet, more… ladylike, as he was always telling her.

As she paced her room, an idea began to form. She could not simply storm into his study; that would be too bold, too reckless. But perhaps she could find another way to learn what was troubling him. Mrs Dunn, her companion, was often privy to the movements of the household staff. If she asked the right questions, she could find out whether her father had been receiving any unusual visitors or letters and who might know more about his recent strange behaviour.

Yes, that was a safer start. She could begin by speaking with Mrs Dunn in the morning, framing her inquiries casually as if she were merely curious about household affairs. If that yielded nothing, perhaps she could find a way to discreetly question Whitmore, the butler. He had been with their family for years and might let something slip if approached delicately.

She gazed out her window into the dark night, the flicker of candlelight from her father's study visible across the courtyard. The one thing she did know was that Mr Hawthorne might be a good match for her father's interests, but for her...

For her, there was only a shrivelled heart and the memory of what might have been.

Chapter Three

THE MURMUR OF VOICES and the soft strains of a quartet welcomed Robert as he stepped onto the expansive lawns of the Bexleys' Hampstead estate. The garden party was in full flourish, guests drifting between clusters of rose bushes and ornate stone statues, each one more elaborately dressed than the last. Robert adjusted his coat, his eyes sweeping the grounds for any sign of Lord Aston. This was not the kind of place he felt at ease, but he had a role to play today.

Hunt had helped him adopt the identity of an investment broker—a man who dealt exclusively with the financial affairs of the wealthy. It was a credible cover; such men were occasionally able to mix in these circles without drawing too much scrutiny... particularly from ladies. With his plain suit and unobtrusive demeanour, Robert appeared just another face among the throng, his presence noted and then quickly forgotten.

He moved through the crowd with calculated ease, nodding to a few curious faces he passed, careful to keep his expression amiable. He was here as a guest, nothing more—a man recently returned to London, reconnecting with old friends and seeking new clients. But beneath this thin veneer of civility, his purpose was clear: observe, listen, and learn.

It did not take long to spot him. Lord Aston stood near a marble fountain, speaking in low tones with a tall, dark-haired man Robert did not recognise. Aston's face was set in a mask of calm, but his posture was rigid, his hand gripping his glass so tightly Robert wondered if it might shatter.

Robert edged closer, pretending to admire the roses that lined the path. The scent of the flowers was sweet, almost cloying, a stark contrast to the bitter tension that gripped his stomach. He positioned himself within earshot, picking up fragments of conversation amid the chatter of the guests.

"—must be discreet," Aston was saying, his voice taut with strain. "We cannot afford any... mistakes."

The dark-haired man nodded, his expression grave. "Of course. But there are risks, especially with the delay."

Aston's eyes darted around, his gaze briefly landing on Robert before moving away. Robert kept his expression neutral, his gaze drifting to the rose petals at his feet. He had to be careful—too much interest would draw suspicion, but he needed to hear more.

"Ensure that it is taken care of," Aston continued, his voice barely above a whisper. "I will not have this hanging over us any longer."

The man nodded again and then slipped away into the crowd. Aston remained by the fountain, his eyes following the man until he disappeared from view. Robert watched as Aston's shoulders slumped slightly, a rare crack in the otherwise impenetrable façade he usually maintained.

Robert turned his attention back to the party, blending into a nearby group discussing the latest political manoeuvres in Parliament. He offered a few well-placed comments, all the while turning over in his mind the fragments of conversation he had overheard. Aston was clearly on edge, and the mention of "risks" and "delays" suggested something more than just social intrigue. But what? And why did Aston look like a man cornered, rather than a man in control?

Then, out of the corner of his eye, he saw *her*.

At first, he thought his mind was playing tricks on him. But there she was—Lady Carmella, moving gracefully through the crowd. The sight of her struck him like a blow. His breath caught in his throat, his heart thudding in his chest. For a moment, he was no longer at the Bexleys' estate, but back at her family's home, the first time he had laid eyes on her. She had been sitting under a great oak tree in the garden, a book open in her lap, her face tilted towards the sun. The memory was as clear as if it had happened yesterday—the way her hair had glinted in the light, the soft curve of her smile as she read.

She had not seen him immediately then, nor had she seen him now. But the mere sight of her, so close yet so unreachable, stirred something deep within him. He had thought he had buried those feelings long ago, thought he had moved past them. But seeing her now, in this place, he felt them all rushing back, overwhelming him like a flood.

He quickly stepped behind a group of laughing ladies, his pulse racing. He could not let her see him. Not here, not now. His last encounter with her on the terrace outside the ball had been brief, but the impact had lingered. She had almost recognised him then, and if she saw him again now, so soon, she might begin to suspect something. And that was a risk he could not afford.

He forced himself to focus, to remember why he was here. This was not the time for distractions, no matter how compelling. But as he watched her move through the crowd, the light catching the emerald green of her gown, he could not help but feel a pang of something he could not name. Regret, perhaps, or longing. Or both.

Carmella reached her father's side, touching his arm gently. "Father, you look rather vexed about something. Are you well?"

Aston startled slightly, then recovered, offering her a tight smile. "I am well, Carmella. Merely... preoccupied. I trust you are enjoying yourself?"

Robert's eyes narrowed. Aston's words were calm, but his expression was anything but. There was a tightness around his mouth, a flicker of something like fear in his eyes. And Carmella, too, seemed to sense it. She nodded, but Robert could see the doubt in her eyes. "Of course, Father, but... Is there anything I can do to help?"

Aston shook his head, his expression closing off. "No. It is nothing you need to concern yourself with. Enjoy the party."

Carmella hesitated, her gaze lingering on her father's face. Then, with a small nod, she turned away, moving back into the flow of the party. Robert watched her go, feeling a deep ache in his chest. She was clearly worried about her father, but he was keeping her at arm's length, shielding her from whatever was troubling him. Something must have changed there, for she used to claim that her father hid nothing from her. That they were close.

Robert clenched his jaw, forcing his gaze away from her. He could not afford to think about her now. He had a job to do—a mission to complete—and he could not let his emotions get in the way. But the sight of her, the sound of her voice, the memory of her sitting under that tree with her book... It was all too much.

It was time to move closer to the core of the conversation. He made his way toward the main pavilion, where refreshments were being served, and positioned himself near a cluster of gentlemen discussing the latest news from the Continent. From here, he had a clear view of Lord Aston, who had moved to a quieter corner of the garden.

As Robert observed from a distance, a young man—one he vaguely remembered as a minor noble with aspirations above his station—drifted towards Aston, his steps hesitant, his demeanour overly cautious. They exchanged a few quiet words, their heads bowed together in an almost casual manner. Only the brief flicker of Aston's narrowed gaze suggested anything amiss. With a swift, almost imperceptible motion, the young man slipped a small envelope into Aston's hand before fading back into the crowd, his departure unremarkable to any but the most observant.

Robert's interest was piqued. Whatever was in that envelope, it had been delivered with a great deal of caution. He decided to follow Aston more closely, but not too closely. He needed to find a way to get a glimpse of what was inside that envelope without alerting Aston to his presence.

As he moved around the garden, carefully shadowing Aston, he could not help but steal another glance at Carmella. She was standing by a cluster of ladies, her head bent in polite conversation, but her eyes kept drifting back to her father. She was worried—he could see it in the way her fingers fidgeted with the lace of her gloves, the way her smile never quite reached her eyes.

He wondered if she had any inkling of what her father was involved in, if she had heard whispers or seen signs. He doubted it. She had always been so sheltered, so protected. But she was clever, and if anyone could sense that something was amiss, it would be her.

He turned his focus back to Aston, watching as the man slipped down a secluded pathway leading to the edge of the garden. Robert waited a few moments, ensuring no one was watching him, then followed quietly.

The path was narrow and winding, the hedges tall and dense. It provided ample cover, but Robert knew he could not afford to be careless. He slowed his steps, moving quietly, his senses alert to any sound or movement. He could see Aston ahead, pausing at a small gazebo. The man glanced around, checking to see if he was alone, then slipped inside.

Robert crept closer, careful to keep his footsteps light. He reached the edge of the hedges, peering through a small gap. He could see Aston inside the gazebo, unfolding the envelope. There was a single sheet of paper inside. Aston read it quickly, his face tightening with every line. When he finished, he crumpled the paper in his hand, his expression a mix of anger and fear.

Robert's curiosity burned. What could have provoked such a reaction? He watched as Aston stuffed the crumpled paper into his pocket and glanced around again before leaving the gazebo and heading back toward the party. Robert stayed hidden until Aston was out of sight, then made his way to the gazebo.

He looked around cautiously before stepping inside. The gazebo was empty, save for the faint scent of tobacco that lingered in the air. Robert's gaze swept over the small, ornate table and the benches, looking for anything that might have been left behind—any clue, however small, that could point him toward what Lord Aston was involved in.

But there was nothing. No papers, no hastily discarded notes, not even a stray piece of sealing wax. Just the pristine surface of the table, the cushions carefully arranged. Whoever had been here before, whether Aston or someone else, had been careful.

Robert felt a wave of frustration rise within him. He had hoped—perhaps foolishly—that Aston might have left some trace, some reply for whomever it was that had sent him that note. But there was nothing. He was grasping at shadows, and the shadows were slipping through his fingers.

He lingered for a moment longer, scanning the floor, the corners, anywhere a clue might hide. But the gazebo was immaculate, offering nothing but a dead end.

It was not much, and that was the problem—it was nothing. He had come away empty-handed, and yet he was plagued with the nagging feeling that something was about to happen. Whatever Lord Aston was hiding, he was good at it. Too good.

He would need to try another approach, be more patient. Perhaps it was time to look elsewhere or listen more carefully. He had a lead now, a sense that something significant was brewing, but he needed more—much more—before he could act.

As he stepped back out into the garden, blending into the crowd once more, he spotted Carmella again. She was still standing by the fountain, her face turned toward the house, lost in thought. For a moment, he considered approaching her, speaking to her, finding out what she knew. But he dismissed the idea just as quickly. He could not involve her in this—not yet. Not when he had nothing to go on.

Instead, he kept his distance, frustration simmering beneath the surface. He had a mission to complete, and he could not afford any distractions or mistakes. Not even her.

CARMELLA STOOD BY THE fountain, her eyes following her father as he moved through the crowd, his expression carefully composed. She watched him greet a group of gentlemen, his gestures polite yet distant, his eyes restless. There was something different about him today, something more guarded. Her mind wandered back to their conversation earlier—how he had evaded her questions, his responses curt and evasive. Whatever was troubling him, he clearly did not want her involved.

She took a deep breath, steadying herself against the unease creeping into her thoughts. She knew her father well, perhaps too well. He was a man who valued control, who thrived in the predictability of his carefully curated life. But lately, she had noticed cracks in his composure, fleeting moments where he seemed genuinely unsettled. She needed to understand why.

Just then, she felt a presence beside her. "Lady Carmella," Roland Hawthorne's voice carried a forced cheerfulness, a charm that always seemed a shade too polished. "You are a vision, as always."

She turned, offering a polite smile. "Thank you, Mr Hawthorne. I trust you are enjoying the party?"

"Indeed, though I find myself more interested in your company," he replied. "Your father seems particularly engaged today. Is there some business on his mind?"

Carmella met his gaze, her smile unwavering. "Father is often preoccupied with matters of business, Mr Hawthorne. It is nothing out of the ordinary."

Roland inclined his head slightly. "Of course, a man in his position would be. Still, I do hope he is not too burdened. After all, we have much to look forward to." His words hung in the air, laden with implication.

She felt a flicker of irritation but kept her expression calm. "One should always look forward, Mr Hawthorne, but I find it just as important to remain present in the moment." Her words were pointed, and she saw his smile falter for a moment, a slight tightening at the corners of his mouth.

"Wise words, indeed," he said, recovering quickly. "Perhaps we might discuss the future over a dance later?"

She gave a gracious nod, her tone even. "Perhaps." With that, she turned away, excusing herself before he could press further.

As she moved through the garden, she noticed several of the ladies gathered around Mrs Dunn, who was regaling them with some tale or another. Carmella approached with a casual air, her steps light on the gravel path.

"Mrs Dunn," she called softly.

Mrs Dunn turned, her face brightening. "Lady Carmella! I was just telling the ladies about our little adventure in Bath last spring. Quite the event, if you recall."

"Yes, quite," Carmella replied with a small smile. "Might I have a word with you in private?"

"Of course, my dear," Mrs Dunn replied, her expression softening with concern. She excused herself from the group, and Carmella led her down a quieter path, out of earshot.

"Mrs Dunn," Carmella began, her voice low, "have you noticed anything unusual with my father lately? Letters, visitors—anything out of the ordinary?"

Mrs Dunn hesitated, glancing around before speaking in a hushed tone. "There have been more letters, my lady. He reads them in his study and then burns them right after. And there was a visitor a few nights ago, after dark. He did not stay long, and I did not see his face."

Carmella's heart quickened. "Did you hear anything at all?"

"No, my lady," Mrs Dunn said. "Only that they spoke in low voices, and your father seemed quite... distracted."

"Thank you, Mrs Dunn. You've been very helpful," Carmella replied, giving her a reassuring smile. She watched as Mrs Dunn returned to the group of ladies, then turned her gaze back toward the garden.

Her father was now speaking with another gentleman, his manner calm, but she could see a tension in the way he held himself—an unnatural stiffness to his normally assured posture. She had never seen him so uneasy before, and it stirred a worry she could not quite name. The sight made her stomach twist with uncertainty. What could be troubling him so?

She continued walking along the path, her thoughts drifting back over half a dozen of their recent conversations. He had seemed almost distracted, his answers clipped and evasive. Her father had always been forthright with her, and this new secretive behaviour felt foreign, unsettling. She wanted to believe there was a reasonable explanation, but the niggling doubt kept pulling at her, urging her to look closer to see if there was something more beneath the surface.

As she wandered further, she noticed a small group of young ladies seated on a nearby bench beneath a canopy of wisteria, their heads bent close together, whispering and giggling. Carmella paused by a cluster of hydrangeas, pretending to admire their vivid blue blooms while letting the light-hearted chatter fill her ears.

Their laughter was a welcome distraction, a reminder of simpler days when such gatherings had been carefree and uncomplicated. "Did you see Lord Bexley's son?" one of the girls said, her voice barely above a whisper. "I hear he's back from the Continent and quite dashing now, much to the delight of Lady Waverly."

"Oh, indeed," another responded with a chuckle. "But everyone knows he's set his sights on Miss Greenfield—his ambitions seem to reach beyond mere flirtation."

Carmella allowed herself a small smile, amused by the trivialities that seemed to captivate her peers. There had been a time when she, too, had found such talk endlessly entertaining, but now it seemed so far removed from anything she could bring herself to care about.

"And what of Lord Aston?" a third girl murmured, her tone curious. "I've heard he's been seen late at night, away from his estate. Some say he's involved in something... unusual."

Carmella's smile faded. Her heart gave a small lurch. She kept her eyes on the flowers, resisting the urge to turn and face the speaker. "Unusual?" another voice echoed. "What do you mean?"

The first girl glanced around before continuing, her voice lowered further. "I don't know the details, but my brother mentioned he's been asking questions in circles he doesn't usually frequent. And there are rumours... of things that are better not spoken of."

Carmella felt her breath catch. Rumours? Strange questions? This wasn't the idle gossip she had expected. She forced herself to remain still, pretending to adjust her shawl as the conversation continued.

"Surely it's nothing," another girl said dismissively. "Lord Aston is a respectable gentleman. People will say anything to amuse themselves."

"Perhaps," the first girl conceded, "but where there is smoke, there is often fire."

Carmella's hand froze mid-adjustment. The words struck a chord of fear in her. Her father, always so conscious of propriety, entangled in rumours? It was hard to fathom. She tried to dismiss it as idle talk, but she couldn't ignore the disquiet it stirred within her.

She took a slow breath, steadying herself before stepping away from the hydrangeas. Her gaze returned to her father, who had now moved toward the far end of the garden, his stride purposeful. She felt a sudden urge to go to him, to ask outright what was going on, but she hesitated. What would she say? And what if he brushed her off again?

Caught in indecision, she glanced around the garden, seeking a distraction, and that was when she saw him—Robert. He stood at the edge of the lawn, partially obscured by the shade of a large oak, his eyes scanning the crowd with an intensity that made her heart skip a beat.

A surge of conflicting emotions rose within her—shock, anger, and a hint of something deeper she dared not name. What was he doing here? She watched him carefully, her breath shallow as she tried to make sense of his presence.

Robert turned slightly, and their eyes met across the distance. Her breath hitched, a rush of memories flooding back, unwanted and unbidden. She saw a flicker of recognition in his gaze, something that made her chest tighten. Before she could react, he turned away, disappearing back into the crowd.

She remained frozen for a moment, her thoughts jumbled, her pulse quickening. Why had he come? Was it a mere coincidence, or was he here for something else? And why, after all this time, did his presence still affect her so deeply?

The voices of the girls nearby brought her back to herself, their chatter a distant hum now. She looked back toward the spot where Robert had been, a new determination forming. Whatever the reason for his return, she needed to find out more. Not just about him, but about her father too.

She turned away, heading back toward the house with a purpose that felt both foreign and necessary. She didn't know what she was looking for exactly, but she knew she couldn't ignore the questions any longer.

Chapter Four

ROBERT SAT IN THE corner of a dimly lit public house, a few miles from the Bexleys' estate. The tavern was unremarkable—exactly the sort of place where a man could sit undisturbed, nursing a drink without drawing attention. A few scattered patrons occupied the room, each lost in their own thoughts or hushed conversations. The low hum of voices and the smell of ale filled the air, providing a stark contrast to the elegance of the garden party he had attended earlier that day. Yet, despite his efforts to blend in, Robert's thoughts were far from the present.

His gaze rested on the half-empty tankard before him, but he wasn't truly seeing it. His mind kept drifting back to the moment he saw her—Carmella—moving through the crowd with that familiar grace, her emerald gown catching the light. He hadn't expected to see her again so soon, not after their brief and unsettling encounter at the ball. The sight of her had been like a punch to the gut, bringing back memories he had fought to bury.

He closed his eyes, letting the memory wash over him—another time he had been this close to her, truly close. It had been in the gardens of her family estate, a place he had come to know well during the summer he spent repairing the stables. They had met by chance—or perhaps not so chance, as he had found himself walking that way more often than not, drawn by some invisible thread that always seemed to lead him to her.

That day had been warm, the sun casting dappled shadows through the leaves of the old oak under which she sat. He remembered the way she had looked up from her book, a soft smile touching her lips as she saw him. She had always been a sight to behold, but in that moment, with the sunlight catching her hair and the hint of laughter in her eyes, she had seemed almost ethereal.

They had talked for a while—about nothing, really. The latest novels she was reading, the peculiar behaviour of the old head gardener, trivial matters that had somehow felt important simply because he was sharing them with her. He had watched her lips move, mesmerised by the way her eyes danced with every word, until the words themselves had become lost in the rhythm of her voice.

And then, as if drawn by a force neither could resist, he had reached for her hand. It had been an impulsive gesture, one that surprised even him. Her fingers had been warm, soft, and for a moment, she had looked at him with such intensity that he had forgotten how to breathe. There had been a beat—a single, electrifying moment where everything hung in the balance. And then, slowly, she had leaned in, her eyes fluttering shut, her breath mingling with his as their lips met in a soft, tentative kiss.

He could still remember the feeling of her lips against his—soft and warm, tasting faintly of honey. He had wanted to pull her closer, to deepen the kiss, but he had held back, afraid to break the fragile spell of the moment. When they finally pulled apart, her cheeks had been flushed, her eyes bright, and he had seen a mix of surprise and wonder in her gaze that mirrored his own.

But that kiss had been the beginning of the end. He should have known then that such a moment could never last. Not for them. Not with the world they lived in, with the rules that governed their every action. They were from different worlds, and though he had dared to dream otherwise, reality had come crashing down soon enough.

Robert opened his eyes, blinking away the memory. His chest ached with the weight of it, with the knowledge of all that had been lost since then. He had tried to forget her, tried to move on, but seeing her today had brought it all back with a vengeance. The way she had looked at him, even from across the garden, had stirred something deep within him—something he thought he had buried.

He took a long sip from his tankard, trying to steady himself, to remind himself why he was here. He had a mission to complete, a duty to fulfil. There were larger matters at stake than his heart's foolish longings. But the memory of that kiss, of the way she had felt in his arms, refused to be silenced.

His thoughts were interrupted by the creaking of the tavern door. A man entered, his eyes scanning the room with a cautious glance. He was rough-looking, with a scruffy beard and the wary posture of someone who knew how to stay out of trouble. Robert's instincts sharpened. The man's gaze landed briefly on him before moving on. He took a seat at the far end of the room, ordering a drink, but his eyes continued to dart around the room.

Robert kept his posture relaxed, his hand hovering near the knife beneath his coat. He knew better than to let his guard down. The man took a long swig from his drink, then, after a moment, made his way over to Robert's table.

"Mind if I join you?" the man asked, his tone casual, but Robert caught the edge of something more—a hint of purpose.

Robert gestured to the empty chair. "Be my guest," he replied evenly.

The man sat down, his eyes studying Robert's face. "Word has it you're looking for something," he said, his voice low. "Or perhaps... someone."

Robert didn't react, keeping his expression neutral. "Word travels fast," he said. "But you shouldn't believe everything you hear."

The man leaned in slightly, lowering his voice. "There's talk of a certain gentleman... a man of influence, who's been moving in some unusual circles lately. Asking questions that don't quite fit."

Robert felt a flicker of interest but kept his features carefully composed. "And why would that concern me?"

The man shrugged. "Might not. But it's the kind of thing that tends to interest certain people—people who like to keep their ears to the ground."

Robert chose his next words carefully. "You seem to have quite the ear yourself."

The man smirked, taking another drink. "I hear things. And sometimes, I see things. I've seen a lot recently—things that might be valuable to the right person."

Robert studied the man, weighing his options. He was clearly fishing, trying to gauge Robert's interest without revealing too much. "And who is this 'gentleman' you're speaking of?"

The man hesitated for a moment, as if deciding how much to reveal. "A lord," he said finally. "A man who's been asking the wrong sorts of questions. Questions that might get him into trouble."

Robert's eyes narrowed slightly. "I see. And what would you want in exchange for this information?"

The man's smile was tight. "Nothing's free in this world. But I think we could come to an arrangement. Meet me tomorrow night, by the old mill on the river. It's quiet there. We can talk more freely."

Robert nodded slowly, understanding the implications. This could be the lead he needed, or it could be a trap. Either way, he had no choice but to follow through. "I'll consider it," he said.

The man finished his drink and stood, his eyes lingering on Robert for a moment. "Do more than consider it," he said quietly. "Time is short, and you might find what you're looking for sooner than you think."

With that, he turned and walked out of the tavern, leaving Robert alone with his thoughts. The man hadn't mentioned Lord Aston by name, but it was clear he knew more than he let on. Robert would have to tread carefully.

He watched the door swing shut behind the man and took a deep breath. He needed to stay focused, to keep his mind clear. He glanced down at his tankard, the memory of Carmella's kiss still fresh in his mind. He couldn't afford distractions—not now, not when so much was at stake. But the thought of her, of her soft touch and the way she had looked at him, lingered like a ghost he couldn't shake.

He closed his eyes for a moment, the noise of the tavern fading away as he let himself remember. He could almost feel her hand in his again, the softness of her lips as they met his under the canopy of stars. A stolen moment, forbidden but cherished. It had been everything, and yet it had led to this—this life of shadows and secrets, far from the world they might have had.

Robert opened his eyes and set down his tankard with a quiet determination. He could not allow himself to be distracted, not now. But the ache remained, deep and unyielding, like an old wound that had never quite healed. He knew what he had to do. But it didn't make the knowing any easier.

With a final glance around the dim room, he rose and walked out into the crisp night air. The chill hit him like a slap, sharpening his senses, grounding him in the present. He pulled his coat tighter, feeling the weight of the choices he had made—the ones that had led him here and the ones he still had to make.

He started down the street, his steps steady, his heart heavier than he would ever admit.

CARMELLA STEPPED THROUGH THE front door of the London townhouse, the echoes of the garden party still whispering in her ears. The lively conversations, the rustle of gowns, the clinking of glasses—it all seemed so far away now. She had left the party early, needing the quiet and solitude of home to clear her mind. Seeing Robert had unsettled her more than she wanted to admit.

As she removed her gloves, she noticed an unusual flurry of activity in the entrance hall. Two footmen were carrying trunks and valises up the grand staircase. A third was struggling with a particularly heavy trunk, nearly losing his grip as he manoeuvred it through the doorway.

"What on earth...?" Carmella began, her brows furrowing. "Whose belongings are these?"

Before the footman could answer, a familiar voice cut through the air. "Ah, Carmella, there you are at last." Aunt Eleanor stood at the top of the staircase, her expression one of mild disapproval, as if Carmella were the one arriving unannounced.

"Aunt Eleanor?" Carmella blinked, surprise colouring her voice. "I didn't know you were coming to stay."

Aunt Eleanor descended the stairs with a measured grace, her dark skirts sweeping the marble steps. "Didn't know? How peculiar. Your father assured me he had informed you of my arrival."

Carmella pressed her lips together, her irritation rising. "He mentioned nothing of it to me," she replied, trying to keep her tone polite. "I would have made preparations otherwise."

"Ah, well, that is rather like your father, isn't it?" Aunt Eleanor said with a dismissive wave of her hand. "So many things on his mind. But no matter, here I am. I trust you will help me settle in and ensure I am well-accommodated."

"Of course," Carmella said, forcing a smile. "You are always welcome, Aunt."

"Indeed," Aunt Eleanor replied, her sharp eyes scanning the house as if searching for faults. "I shall also be assisting in overseeing your social engagements while I'm here. There are certain expectations, after all, and I intend to ensure that you are making the most of your season."

Carmella's smile tightened. "How thoughtful of you," she said, though the thought of Aunt Eleanor managing her social calendar made her stomach twist with frustration. Her aunt's arrival meant stricter supervision and less freedom to pursue her own interests, whatever they might be.

As Aunt Eleanor continued to issue instructions to the servants, Carmella took a deep breath, trying to quell her annoyance. Why hadn't her father mentioned Aunt Eleanor's visit? And why now, of all times? Her father's behaviour had been so strange lately—distracted, secretive. And now this unexpected intrusion.

"Aunt Eleanor," Carmella ventured, "I don't suppose Father mentioned why he invited you to stay?"

Aunt Eleanor paused, turning to face her. "He said he had some matters to attend to and thought it best I keep you company in his absence. As for why, you'll have to ask him yourself." She gave a thin smile. "And, of course, I'm here to help guide you in certain... matters."

Carmella nodded, though she felt no clearer than before. Her father's sudden desire for Aunt Eleanor's presence only added to her growing list of concerns. "Well, I hope you find everything to your liking," she said, keeping her tone light. "If you'll excuse me, I think I shall retire for the evening."

Aunt Eleanor gave a curt nod. "Very well. We shall speak more in the morning. There are certain things I wish to discuss with you—about your prospects and your future. But for now, rest. You look as if you've had a... a wonderful day, my dear."

Carmella turned, biting back a retort. She made her way up the stairs, her thoughts a whirlwind of frustration. The moment she reached her room, she closed the door with a soft click and leaned against it, exhaling deeply. Her father's secretive behaviour, the unexpected appearance of Aunt Eleanor, and then Robert—oh, Robert, of all people to see today. It was too much.

She moved to the window, pushing aside the heavy drapes to stare out into the darkened street below. The lamplights flickered in the distance, casting long shadows on the cobblestones. She had been so unprepared for Robert's sudden reappearance in her life, so caught off guard by the emotions it stirred in her. She hadn't allowed herself to think of him—really think of him—in months. And yet, seeing him today, even from a distance, had brought it all rushing back.

Her fingers tightened around the edge of the drape, her mind drifting back to the last time she had seen him, really seen him—the night he left. She could still hear his voice, thick with emotion, telling her that he had to go, that he couldn't be what she needed, what she deserved. The memory was as sharp as a knife, cutting through the fog of her thoughts. She had watched him walk away, her heart breaking with each step he took.

And now he was back. *Why?* What could he possibly want?

A knock at her door broke her thoughts. She opened it to find a maid standing there, looking a bit hesitant. "Begging your pardon, my lady," the maid said, "but your aunt wishes to see you in her room."

Carmella sighed. "Very well. Tell her I'll be there shortly." As the maid curtsied and left, Carmella straightened her shoulders, preparing herself for whatever Aunt Eleanor might have to say.

Moments later, she knocked softly on her aunt's door. "Come in," came the brisk reply.

Carmella entered to find Aunt Eleanor sitting in a high-backed chair, a cup of tea in her hand. "I hope I'm not disturbing you," Carmella began, though she knew her aunt had summoned her.

"Not at all," Aunt Eleanor said, gesturing to a chair across from her. "I thought we might have a little chat before retiring. It seems there are a few things we need to discuss."

Carmella took a seat, smoothing her skirts. "Of course. What is it you wish to discuss, Aunt?"

Aunt Eleanor sipped her tea, her eyes sharp over the rim of the cup. "Your father, for one," she said, setting the cup down. "He seems... rather preoccupied of late. More so than usual. Have you noticed?"

Carmella nodded slowly. "Yes, I have. He's been very secretive, especially these past few weeks. I'm worried about him."

Aunt Eleanor leaned forward slightly. "As am I. Which is why I'm here. He asked me to keep an eye on things, particularly you. It seems he has some pressing matters to attend to, and he did not want you left unattended."

Carmella bristled slightly at the implication but held her tongue. "Do you know what these matters are?"

Aunt Eleanor shook her head. "No, he was quite vague, as is his habit. But he did make it clear that you were to be guided accordingly. And I must say, Carmella, you have been far too independent of late. It is time you started thinking seriously about your future—about making a suitable match."

Carmella sighed inwardly. She knew where this was heading. "If you're referring to Roland Hawthorne—"

"Yes, I am," Aunt Eleanor interrupted. "He is a perfectly respectable gentleman with good prospects."

"He has no title," Carmella reminded her. "I was always told that was the first qualification in any suitor I considered."

"Do not be sharp with me, child. There are more considerations than having a title. Your father and I both agree that Hawthorne would make an excellent match for you."

"But what if that is not what I want?"

Aunt Eleanor's expression softened slightly, but her tone remained firm. "Sometimes, my dear, we must think beyond our own desires. We must consider what is best for the family, for our future. I know you..." Aunt Eleanor cleared her throat. "Two years ago, you fancied yourself quite taken with some... ruffian..."

Carmella's head snapped up. "He was no ruffian!"

"He was no gentleman," her aunt retorted firmly. "I know not the nature of your... attachment... but thank heaven, no real harm was done. Your father managed to hush up whatever... indiscretions you may have carried on, and for that, you must thank your lucky stars."

"Must I?"

Her aunt levelled a stare at her. "You think your father has not noticed how you were altered after that? That I did not see it? Child, you really are naive. Yes, you ought to count yourself fortunate that your father was looking out for your interests and that no one in society was the wiser. It is time to turn your thoughts to more... mature reflections. Those befitting a lady of rank, not some scullery girl."

Carmella looked down, her hands clenched in her lap. "Scullery girls at least have some liberties in choosing their lives," she said quietly.

"You think that, do you?" Her aunt snorted. "Perhaps you ought to sit and speak with one sometime." Aunt Eleanor sighed, her expression softening a little. "I understand more than you think, Carmella. There was a time when I, too, had to make a choice between love and duty. I chose duty, and I do not regret it, but it was not easy. Sometimes, we must make sacrifices for the greater good."

Carmella looked up, surprised by the confession. She had never thought of her aunt as anything other than the stern, practical woman she had always known. "You loved someone?"

Aunt Eleanor nodded, a distant look in her eyes. "Yes, once. But it was not meant to be. And I made my peace with that long ago. You must do the same."

Carmella swallowed, her mind a whirl of thoughts. She had never considered that her aunt might have had her own regrets, her own lost loves. It made her see Aunt Eleanor in a new light, but it didn't make the decision any easier. Silence settled between them, heavy with unspoken thoughts. Carmella's mind churned with questions about her father and her future. Her gaze drifted to the dim light under the door, the faint glow from the hallway seeping into the room.

Aunt Eleanor took another sip of her tea, her expression thoughtful. "Your father has been rather occupied these days," she said, her tone casual but her eyes watching Carmella closely. "But that is not unusual for a man in his position."

Carmella nodded slowly, though unease still nagged at her. She tried to reassure herself that her father's late nights were just part of his responsibilities, nothing more. But the secrecy, the evasiveness—it wasn't like him. He had always been a man of honour, a man who dealt plainly, even with his daughter.

"I just... I wonder what could be troubling him so," Carmella murmured, half to herself, her fingers twisting in her lap.

Aunt Eleanor set her cup down with a soft clink. "Men often carry burdens they do not share with their families, Carmella," she said. "Especially with females. We must trust that your father knows what he is doing and that he is handling whatever matters concern him."

Carmella glanced at her aunt, seeing the hint of worry in her eyes despite her composed demeanour. It was clear Aunt Eleanor, too, had noticed the change in her brother, though she would never admit it outright.

"Yes, of course," Carmella replied, though her heart still felt heavy.

Aunt Eleanor reached out, gently squeezing Carmella's hand. "Try not to fret, my dear. Worrying will do no good. Your father is a capable man, and he will see to whatever needs handling."

Carmella nodded again, trying to take comfort in her aunt's words. Yet, as she left her aunt's room and walked down the hall to her own, her mind refused to quiet. She paused at the top of the staircase, glancing down toward her father's study door. It remained closed, a thin line of light beneath it.

She hesitated, feeling a pull to go down, to knock and ask her father directly what was troubling him. But she knew it would be futile; he would only tell her not to concern herself, that everything was well. And so, with a sigh, she turned and made her way to her room, deciding it was best to let it be for now.

Chapter Five

ROBERT HAD RETURNED TO his modest lodgings, a small room above a cooper's shop in a less travelled part of London. The single candle on the desk cast flickering shadows across the walls, its light barely reaching the corners of the narrow space. The room was sparse—a narrow bed against the wall, a rough-hewn chair, and a small desk littered with papers, a half-eaten loaf of bread, and a dented tin cup. It was enough for his needs, though hardly comfortable.

He leaned forward, methodically inspecting the contents of his haversack, the leather worn but sturdy. Inside, he had a few essential items: a coil of thin rope, a small tinderbox, a flask of water, and a pouch of dried meat. He checked his weapons next, ensuring his pistol was loaded and his knife sharp. He adjusted the blade in his boot, making certain it was secure but accessible. Each item was carefully chosen, each piece of equipment serving a purpose. He could not afford any mistakes tonight.

As he worked, his mind was far from steady. The memory of Carmella's face at the garden party kept intruding, breaking his concentration. He could still see the way she had looked at him, her eyes wide with a mix of shock, hurt, and something deeper—something he dared not name. She had seen him, he was sure of it. She had recognised him despite the shadows, despite the distance. The realisation filled him with both dread and a twisted sense of hope.

That was twice now that he had inadvertently caught her notice. The first might have been forgotten or written off as a moment of fancy—too much punch and the night too dark, something of that nature. But this second time... that was sheer carelessness. And Carmella was too inquisitive to brush it off without a thought.

That was... *if* she still thought of him. Did she? He had promised to find a way to be worthy of her, to win her hand, but after two years of being in the world, seeing the way of things, well... he was fooling himself. Even if he won battle honours and medals with fringed epaulettes at his shoulders and the Prince's own blessing on his brow, he would never be more than a man who stepped out of his circles.

Perhaps, in the last two years, Carmella had come to understand that. Perhaps she had forgot all about him. A pity he could not do the same.

"Blast," he muttered under his breath, setting the pistol down with a sharp clatter. He was supposed to be focusing on the mission, not allowing himself to be distracted by memories or emotions. But seeing her again had stirred up everything he had tried to bury—the longing, the regret, the love that had never truly faded.

He shook his head, trying to clear his thoughts. There was no room for that now. He pulled on a dark wool coat, the fabric rough against his skin, and fastened the buttons carefully. He would blend into the night, become a shadow among shadows.

His gaze fell on the corner of the desk where a small, nearly forgotten keepsake lay—a single button from Carmella's gown. He had found it, half buried in the mud two years ago before she had left for London, after their last encounter in the gardens. He had kept it all this time, a foolish memento of a life he could never have. He reached for it now, his fingers brushing against the smooth, worn surface.

A soft knock at the door broke the silence, and his hand flew to the knife at his belt. "Who is it?" he called, keeping his voice low.

"It's Hunt," came the reply, the familiar voice of his former captain. Robert relaxed, his hand dropping from the blade. He moved to the door and opened it cautiously, letting the older man inside.

Hunt entered with a nod, his eyes sweeping the room. "Thought I'd find you here," he said quietly, his tone a mixture of concern and camaraderie. "Word has it you've been asking questions. Not everyone's happy about it."

Robert closed the door behind him, nodding. "I've been careful."

"Careful enough?" Hunt raised an eyebrow, crossing his arms. "The wrong people are starting to notice. You need to watch your back, Daniels."

Robert gave a tight smile. "I always do."

Hunt studied him for a moment, sensing something on Robert's mind. "What are you planning? You've got that look about you."

Robert hesitated, then decided to confide in him. "I've arranged a meeting tonight. The old mill by the river."

Hunt's expression darkened with concern. "A secluded place like that... sounds like a perfect spot for an ambush."

Robert nodded. "I know. But the informant might have the lead we need. I can't afford to pass it up."

Hunt frowned, clearly uneasy. "You want backup? I can be nearby, keep an eye out."

Robert shook his head. "No, the man's skittish. If he thinks I've brought anyone, he'll bolt. I have to go alone."

"Very well, but be smart about it. And signal if you need help. Don't try to handle it all on your own."

Robert smirked. "I'm no hero, Hunt. Just trying to do my job."

Hunt clapped him on the shoulder. "Just remember, a dead man can't finish the job. Be smart, Daniels."

Robert nodded, his expression sobering. "I will."

As Hunt left, Robert took a deep breath, steadying himself. He had to focus. He couldn't afford to let his emotions cloud his judgment. He grabbed his haversack, slinging it over his shoulder, and slipped out into the night.

The streets of London were quiet at this hour, a thin fog settling over the cobblestones, muffling his footsteps. He moved quickly but carefully, avoiding the main roads and sticking to the shadows of narrow alleyways and side streets.

He reached the edge of the river, the old mill looming ahead, its silhouette dark against the cloudy night sky. He paused, crouching behind a low stone wall, and surveyed the area. The mill was dilapidated, its wooden beams sagging with age, the door hanging slightly ajar. It was the perfect place for a clandestine meeting—or an ambush.

He waited, his breath steady, his eyes scanning the shadows. The river murmured softly beside him, a faint mist rising from its surface. He could see no one, but his instincts told him he was not alone. He knew better than to trust appearances. He would have to move carefully.

After a few minutes, a shadow detached itself from the darkness near the mill and moved cautiously toward the entrance. The informant. Robert watched as the man glanced around, his posture tense, before slipping inside the mill.

Robert waited a moment longer, then moved. He kept low, his footsteps silent against the damp earth, his body blending into the darkness. He reached the mill door and slipped inside, his eyes adjusting to the dim interior. The informant stood in the centre of the room, his back to Robert, clearly on edge.

"Who's there?" the man called out, his voice wavering.

"Someone who wants answers," Robert replied evenly, stepping into view. The informant spun around, his eyes wide with fear.

"Don't shoot!" the man cried, raising his hands. "I'm unarmed!"

Robert's expression remained hard, his gaze fixed on the informant. The man had seemed so cocky in the tavern, but here, tonight, he was skittish as a hare. Something must have happened since yesterday. "You've got information," he said, his tone steady, giving nothing away. "Start talking."

The man swallowed hard, his eyes darting around the dimly lit mill. "I—I don't know much," he stammered. "There's been talk... someone high up, with influence. A lord, I think. Someone's been asking questions, making moves that don't add up."

Robert's pulse quickened, but he kept his expression neutral. "A name," he demanded. "I need a name."

The informant shifted nervously, his face pale in the moonlight filtering through the broken window. "I don't know for sure, but... I've heard whispers. Lord Aston. They say he's been seen meeting with some... questionable types. Rumours about secrets, things being passed to the French."

Robert felt a chill run down his spine. *Aston.* The name was confirmed now, but it wasn't enough to act on—yet. "Who's behind this?" he pressed. "Who's paying you?"

The informant trembled, his voice barely more than a whisper. "I don't know. The money comes from a middleman, always the same. I never met the real buyer. Just a name—Breck. He handles the dirty work."

Breck... one of Owen North's old contacts. This Breck was his next lead, but the informant wasn't giving him enough. "Why tell me this now?" he asked, his voice edged with suspicion.

The man's eyes widened with desperation. "I need your help," he confessed, his voice trembling. "This... it's bigger than I thought, and I don't want any part of it anymore. They're watching me. If I try to run on my own, they'll catch me before I'm out of London. I thought... if I told you something useful, you might help me get out of the city—get me to Scotland."

Robert studied him for a long moment, weighing his options. The informant seemed genuinely afraid, trapped in a situation beyond his control. Helping him escape could be risky, but it might be the only way to get more information. "Why should I trust you?" Robert asked quietly.

"Because I've got nothing left to lose," the man replied, his voice raw with fear. "They're already onto me. If I stay, I'm dead. If I go, I need a safe way out. I can't do it alone. Please, just help me get to Scotland. I swear, I'll tell you everything I know."

Robert considered this, the tension thick in the air. He could sense the man's desperation, his fear. Finally, he gave a curt nod. "Very well. I'll get you out of London—but you'd better make it worth my while."

The informant sagged with relief. "Thank you. I swear, I'll tell you everything. Just get me out of here."

Robert motioned for him to stay quiet. "Meet me tomorrow night, at the bridge near the old warehouse. If you're not there, or if I see anyone else, the deal's off."

The informant nodded quickly. "I'll be there, I promise. Just... please, don't let them find me."

Robert watched him go, the unease settling deeper in his chest. He had a name, a hint of a lead—but nothing concrete, nothing that could unravel the full mystery. And yet, this second mention of Aston's name was enough to confirm his darkest suspicions. He knew now that he wasn't imagining things, that there was a reason his instincts had brought him back here.

As he made his way back through the shadowed streets, his mind was a storm of thoughts. If Aston was involved—or being framed—then Carmella was in the middle of something dangerous. And there was still so much he didn't know.

He couldn't shake the feeling that he was being drawn into a trap, each step pulling him deeper into the shadows. He walked on, not sure what he was walking towards—only knowing that whatever it was, it had the power to destroy everything he'd ever wanted.

T HE MORNING SUN CAST a soft, golden light through the curtains of Carmella's bedroom, but she barely noticed. She sat by her window, staring out into the garden below, her thoughts tangled and restless. The birds chirped merrily, and the flowers bloomed in bright colours, but none of it could ease the disquiet in her heart.

She hadn't slept well—not since the garden party. Not since she'd seen Robert again. Twice now, she had caught sight of him. The first time, a shadow at the ball, she had nearly convinced herself it was just a trick of the light, her mind playing tricks on her in a moment of weakness. But at the Bexleys' garden party, she knew she hadn't imagined it. She had seen him clearly, standing amongst the guests, his eyes finding hers with a look she could never forget.

Her heart clenched at the memory. What was he doing back in London? And why now, after all this time? Did he still think of her as she thought of him, or had he moved on, found someone else, someone more suitable? She shook her head, trying to banish the thoughts. She had more pressing concerns—her father's strange behaviour, the pressure from Aunt Eleanor to accept Roland Hawthorne's proposal, and the locked drawer she had discovered in her father's study.

She sighed, rising from her seat. There was no use in brooding. She needed to clear her head, to focus. Aunt Eleanor would be expecting her for breakfast, and it would not do to appear distracted or out of sorts.

She made her way to the dining room, where Aunt Eleanor was already seated, her back straight as a rod, her hands delicately holding a teacup. "Good morning, Aunt," Carmella said, forcing a smile as she took her seat.

"Good morning, dear," Aunt Eleanor replied, her tone clipped. "I trust you slept well?"

"As well as can be expected," Carmella answered, reaching for a slice of toast. She wasn't in the mood for a heavy breakfast, but she knew better than to let Aunt Eleanor see her reluctance. Her aunt had a knack for noticing inconvenient sentiment.

They ate in silence for a few moments, the only sounds the clink of silverware against china and the soft rustle of the morning paper in Aunt Eleanor's hands. Finally, Aunt Eleanor spoke, her voice sharp. "I was thinking, Carmella, it might be prudent for us to arrange a meeting with Mr Hawthorne. He has been most patient, but it would be good to give him some encouragement, don't you think?"

Carmella's grip tightened on her fork. She had no desire to see Roland Hawthorne, not now, not ever. But she knew better than to openly defy her aunt. "Perhaps," she said cautiously, "though I am not sure I am ready to make any decisions just yet."

Aunt Eleanor frowned. "Carmella, you must understand that time is of the essence. Your father has been very clear about his wishes, and it is not wise to delay. Mr Hawthorne is a respectable gentleman with good prospects. You would do well to consider his suit."

Carmella bit back a retort, swallowing her frustration. "I will think on it," she repeated, hoping to end the conversation.

Aunt Eleanor's eyes narrowed slightly, but she nodded. "Very well. But do not take too long. Your father is under enough strain as it is."

Carmella's heart clenched at the mention of her father. "Yes, I know," she said softly, her gaze dropping to her plate. "He has been acting... strangely of late."

Aunt Eleanor set down her teacup, her expression firm. "We have spoken of this enough. Your father has many responsibilities, Carmella. It is not for us to question his actions."

Carmella nodded, though her mind was far from settled. She needed answers, and she couldn't rely on her father or her aunt to provide them. She had to find out for herself.

After breakfast, she excused herself and made her way to the garden, hoping the fresh air would help clear her thoughts. The morning was cool, a gentle breeze rustling the leaves of the trees. She wandered along the paths, her mind turning over the events of the past few days.

As she passed by her father's study, she noticed the door was slightly ajar again. Her heart quickened. She glanced around, ensuring no one was watching, then slipped inside. The room was dimly lit, the curtains drawn to keep out the morning sun. She moved quietly, her eyes scanning the desk for any sign of the key. Unlikely—if her father kept the drawer locked, he would keep the key on his person, but perhaps there was something else...

There *was* a broken seal on something, half-concealed beneath a pile of papers. She reached for it, her hand trembling slightly. But just as her fingers brushed the edge of the letter, she heard footsteps approaching. Her heart leapt into her throat, and she quickly withdrew, retreating to the door. She peered out into the hallway, relieved to see only a maid passing by, carrying linens.

She exhaled slowly, her pulse still racing. She couldn't risk being caught. She would have to find another way to uncover the truth.

L ATER THAT AFTERNOON, AS she sat in the parlour, a familiar face appeared at the door. "Lady Abigail!" Carmella exclaimed, rising to greet her friend. "What a pleasant surprise."

Lady Abigail smiled warmly, embracing Carmella. "I thought I might call on you, see how you were faring."

Carmella nodded, leading her friend to the settee. "Of course. I'm so glad you came. I could use the company. Tea?"

"That would be lovely! But what I really came for was a good bit of gossip. I understand Roland Hawthorne has made his intentions quite clear."

"He... he has."

"Oh, I know that look. You are reluctant? Well, I cannot understand why. Simply half this year's debutantes are wild with envy. But perhaps you know something they do not?" Lady Abigail shot her a sly look over her tea cup.

Carmella hesitated for a moment. "Abigail, have you... heard anything in society? Not about Hawthorn. About my father, I mean. He has been acting rather... peculiar of late."

Lady Abigail's eyes flickered with curiosity. She lowered her voice slightly, leaning closer. "Well, there have been a few whispers, you know how the ladies love to talk. Some say your father has been seen about town with people outside his usual circles. Naturally, tongues are wagging."

Carmella's brow furrowed. "Seen with whom?"

Abigail's lips pressed into a faint smile. "There's been some speculation—completely unsubstantiated, mind you—that he might have taken a fancy to someone. You know how the more imaginative minds will jump to conclusions about a mistress."

Carmella's heart skipped a beat, a mix of embarrassment and disbelief flooding through her. "A mistress? But surely that's just idle talk."

Abigail shrugged, giving a small, knowing smile. "Oh, likely so. You know how society loves a scandal where none exists. But the fact remains, people have noticed a change in him. He seems... preoccupied. Whatever it is, I'm sure there's a perfectly reasonable explanation."

Carmella nodded, though her unease deepened. She knew her father well enough to doubt such gossip, but she couldn't ignore the fact that he had been different—distracted, secretive.

Lady Abigail leaned back, watching Carmella carefully. "Are you worried, my dear? About what people are saying?"

Carmella hesitated, choosing her words with care. "I suppose... I'm more concerned about Father himself. He has been so distant lately, so... unlike himself."

Abigail reached out, placing a reassuring hand on Carmella's arm. "I understand. It must be unsettling. But, Carmella, you know how men can be at times. They have their affairs—both business and otherwise—and they keep their secrets. It's not always our place to pry."

Carmella offered a thin smile. "Yes, I suppose you're right. Still, I wish I could help him, if only he would let me."

Abigail gave her arm a gentle squeeze. "You have a kind heart, Carmella. Perhaps you might find a quiet moment to speak with him, let him know you're here for him. Sometimes, that is all one can do."

Carmella nodded again, her thoughts still churning. "Thank you, Abigail. You always know just what to say."

Lady Abigail smiled softly. "That's what friends are for, isn't it? Besides, I've heard enough scandal for one day. Let's turn our minds to something more pleasant—like the charity event in a fortnight. I've been thinking about the flowers. Perhaps we could use some of the lilies from your garden?"

Carmella seized the change in subject with relief, though her mind lingered on her father. "Yes, I think that would be lovely. The lilies have been blooming beautifully this year."

As they continued discussing the event, Carmella felt a small measure of comfort in the familiarity of their friendship, though the worry about her father remained, like a shadow just out of sight. She knew she would have to do something, but what? And when?

T HAT EVENING, AS CARMELLA prepared for bed, her thoughts drifted back to the conversation with Lady Abigail. The gossip about her father having a mistress was absurd, surely. Yet, there had been a note of something in Abigail's voice—concern, perhaps, or a hint of something unspoken. It had unsettled Carmella, leaving her with a sense that there was more to her father's recent preoccupation than she understood.

As she brushed her hair by the candlelight, she tried to push the thought away, telling herself she was merely frustrated with him over his insistence on this marriage to Roland Hawthorne. That, surely, was the reason for her unease. She was projecting her own dissatisfaction onto her father, seeing things that weren't there.

She paused, setting down her brush, and stared into the mirror. But then her mind began to recount certain oddities she had noticed recently—small things, but enough to unsettle her. Her father had never been one for locked drawers, for instance. He had always kept his papers openly on his desk, without a hint of secrecy. But now there was a locked drawer, and she had seen a small key hanging on his watch chain earlier that day. What could it open?

She shook her head, chiding herself for being fanciful. It was probably nothing, she thought. Just private papers or correspondence. And yet... she found herself wondering. Her father had been so distracted lately, so unlike himself. He had been coming home late, his expression drawn and worried, speaking in vague terms about "matters of business."

She frowned, recalling how he had even seemed to avoid her questions, changing the subject whenever she pressed him about his days. No, this was not just her frustration talking. There was something more. Her father truly was behaving strangely.

She wasn't one to pry, but the idea nagged at her. What could be so important that it must be kept locked away? It wasn't in his nature to keep things hidden. Or at least, it hadn't been. She wondered again about the drawer in his study. Had it always been there? And why would it suddenly be locked now?

Her brow furrowed as she tried to piece it together. Perhaps it was nothing. Perhaps she was making something out of nothing, letting her imagination run wild. But no matter how she tried to dismiss it, the sense of unease lingered.

She turned back to the window, staring out at the darkening sky. Perhaps she was letting her imagination get the better of her, but she couldn't shake the feeling that something wasn't right. Maybe, when the opportunity presented itself, she might take a closer look in her father's study—not out of defiance or a need to pry, but out of concern and curiosity. After all, she only wanted to help.

Chapter Six

T HE HOUR WAS LATE when Robert found himself back in his room above the cooper's shop, though the space now felt smaller, more stifling than before. The air was thick with the scent of old wood and smoke from the chimney below, seeping through the cracks in the floorboards. He had scarcely set foot inside before he tore off his coat and flung it over the back of the chair. His movements were sharper tonight, driven by a restlessness that bordered on agitation.

The map of London lay unfurled on the table, corners weighted down by a pistol, a battered tin cup, and a haphazardly folded shirt. But Robert hardly looked at it. He knew the routes by heart. His eyes were instead fixed on the window, the thin curtains fluttering slightly in the cold draft. The streets below were cloaked in shadows, but his mind was elsewhere, moving through them with a speed and urgency that belied his outward stillness.

And then, as if conjured by some cruel trick of fate, Carmella's face filled his mind again. Not the calm, composed mask she wore before others, but the vulnerable, almost broken expression she had worn at the garden party, when their eyes had met across the expanse. He could still see the way her lips had parted, as though on the verge of speaking, and the flash of recognition—too quick, too subtle for anyone else to notice, but unmistakable to him.

He turned away from the window, clenching his fists until his nails bit into his palms. Why did she have to be part of this? For two years, he had steeled himself against such distractions, burying every tender thought beneath layers of duty and resolve. Yet here he was, teetering on the brink, torn between his mission and the phantom of a past that refused to let go.

A soft knock on the door pulled him abruptly from his thoughts. He drew his knife instinctively, his heart pounding in his chest. The sound was familiar, a hesitant tapping that spoke more of urgency than danger.

"Who is it?" he demanded, his voice rougher than he intended.

"It's Hunt."

Robert sheathed the knife, feeling a sudden wave of relief mixed with irritation. He opened the door to find Captain Hunt standing there, his expression unreadable, though the lines on his face seemed deeper than usual.

"You look terrible," Hunt observed, stepping inside without waiting for an invitation. "Have you slept at all?"

Robert shook his head, not trusting himself to speak.

Hunt's eyes swept over the room, lingering on the map, the haphazard preparations. "What of the informant you met last night?"

"Seems sincere, and terrified. He wants me to get him out of London in exchange for information. I'm to meet him at the bridge."

"The one by the old warehouse?"

Robert nodded curtly. "The informant's jittery, but if he knows anything, it could change everything. I can't ignore it."

"And if it's a setup? If they're leading you into a trap?"

"I know the risks," Robert replied sharply. "But I have to try. If there's even a chance—"

"A chance for what, Daniels?" Hunt cut in, his voice rising with uncharacteristic frustration. "To play the hero? To get yourself killed for a scrap of information that may be worthless?"

Robert's jaw tightened. "I'm not playing at anything. This is bigger than you or me. If I can get to the bottom of this—"

"I cannot help you."

Robert's gaze sharpened. "I never asked you to."

"I know, but I wanted to make sure you understood. I'm leaving London this very hour to return home. This... whatever this is... don't get in over your head. There's no team to back you up this time."

Robert set his jaw. "I know."

Hunt's hand rested briefly on his shoulder, a gesture of both reassurance and resignation. "Be careful, Daniels. You're no good to anyone dead."

As Hunt left, Robert stood motionless for a long moment, the room around him a blur of shadows and half-formed thoughts. He could hear his own breathing, harsh and uneven, like the sound of someone drowning. Slowly, he forced himself to move, to gather his things.

But as he slung the haversack over his shoulder and slipped into the darkened streets, he couldn't shake the feeling that tonight, something was bound to change. Whether for better or worse, he could not say. He only knew that he was walking a razor's edge, and that one wrong step could send him plummeting into an abyss from which there would be no return.

He moved through the narrow streets, keeping to the shadows, his senses alert for any sign of danger. The city was quieter now, the usual hustle and bustle of the day replaced by an eerie stillness. He knew these streets well, knew where to step to avoid making noise, where to hide if necessary. He felt the familiar rush of adrenaline coursing through his veins, heightening his senses.

As he approached the rendezvous point, he felt a prickle of awareness. He slowed his pace, scanning the area. There, just beyond the corner, a figure moved—a shadow in the dark, following him. Robert's instincts flared. Someone was tailing him.

He ducked into a narrow alley, pressing himself against the wall, watching. The figure hesitated at the corner, peering into the darkness. Robert's hand tightened around his pistol, his mind racing. Who could it be? A rival? Someone from the higher-ups, sent to watch him? Or was it connected to the informant's panicked warnings?

The figure lingered a moment longer, then moved on, disappearing into the shadows. Robert exhaled slowly, his grip loosening. He would have to be even more cautious. Whoever was following him could jeopardise the entire operation.

He took a roundabout route to the bridge, careful to avoid any more tails. When he finally reached the meeting point, he stayed hidden in the shadows, watching the surrounding area. The old warehouse loomed nearby, its windows dark, its doors shut tight. The river flowed quietly below, a soft murmur in the night.

After a few tense moments, the informant appeared, hurrying toward the bridge with quick, nervous steps. Robert stepped out of the shadows, raising a hand to signal him. The informant flinched but moved closer, his face pale and drawn.

"You came," the man said, his voice trembling. "I didn't think you would."

Robert's expression remained hard. "I'm here. Now tell me what you know—and quickly. We don't have much time."

The informant swallowed, glancing around nervously. "They're watching me," he whispered. "I'm not safe here. They know I've been talking."

Robert's eyes narrowed. "Who's 'they'?"

The informant shook his head. "I don't know for sure. Just... people with power. People who don't want the truth getting out. I need to get out of London, out of their reach. Can you help me?"

Robert felt a surge of frustration. "I need information, not excuses. Who's behind this? What do you know about Lord Aston?"

The informant's eyes darted nervously. "I only know what they told me to say—to spread rumours, to make people think he's involved with the French. But I don't know if it's true. Please, you have to get me out of here. They'll kill me if I stay."

Before Robert could press further, he heard the faint sound of footsteps—several pairs, approaching fast. His heart leapt, and he grabbed the informant's arm. "We're leaving. Now."

They slipped into the shadows, moving swiftly through the narrow alleys, Robert leading the way. His mind raced. Who had followed them? Was it the same person from earlier or someone else entirely?

As they rounded a corner, a carriage sped past, its wheels clattering on the cobblestones. Robert pulled the informant into a narrow gap between two buildings, holding his breath as the carriage rolled by. He caught a glimpse of the occupants—men with hard eyes, searching, hunting.

Once the carriage had passed, Robert moved again, taking a circuitous route to avoid any further encounters. They finally reached a small, hidden cottage on the outskirts of the city—a safe house he had used before. Robert barricaded the door, turning to face the informant, who was visibly shaking.

"You're safe for now," Robert said, his voice low and steady. "But I need answers—now more than ever."

The informant nodded, his face pale with fear. "I'll tell you everything I know. Just... please, get me to Scotland. Get me out of this city."

Robert studied him, his mind weighing the options. He didn't trust the man, not completely, but he needed the information. And if this was the only way to get it, then so be it. "We'll talk in the morning," he said finally. "For now, get some rest. You'll need it."

As he watched the informant settle into the corner of the room, Robert's thoughts drifted once more to Carmella. If she knew he was back... if she suspected anything... he would need to find a way to keep her safe, too, without getting her involved.

He stared out the small window, watching the darkened streets. The night was far from over, and he knew the real danger was just beginning.

T HE MORNING LIGHT FILTERED softly through the tall windows of the Aston townhouse, casting delicate patterns on the polished floor. Carmella sat at her writing desk, a fine sheet of paper laid out before her, but her quill hesitated, hovering uncertainly above the page. She had been attempting to write a letter to a distant cousin for nearly an hour, but her thoughts were as scattered as the ink blots marring the once pristine parchment. Her mind was elsewhere, tangled in a web of worry and frustration.

The past few days had been a whirlwind, stirring up emotions Carmella had long thought buried. Lady Abigail's attempts to console her had instead unsettled her, planting seeds of doubt that now threatened to sprout uncontrollably. Her father's sudden insistence on her marriage to Roland Hawthorne weighed heavily on her, but was her own restlessness to blame? She had always prided herself on being rational, level-headed, not one to indulge in fanciful notions or the idle gossip of the ton. Yet, here she was, feeling as if her life was spiraling out of her control.

She laid down the quill and leaned back in her chair, her gaze drifting to the window where the early sunlight danced on the glass. Perhaps it was not her father who was being unreasonable, but her own heart rebelling against the life she had been bred to lead. She felt torn—caught between the dutiful daughter she had always been and a woman who yearned for more, who desired something beyond the carefully arranged existence laid out before her. The garden party, the hushed whispers of her friends, and, most unsettling of all, the sight of Robert lurking in the shadows, had all conspired to stir a longing she had tried hard to suppress.

Carmella sighed, pushing herself up from the desk. She crossed the room to the tall window, her fingers brushing the cool glass as she looked out over the gardens below. The roses were in full bloom, their scent drifting faintly upwards, but she found no comfort in their beauty today. Instead, her thoughts kept drifting back to the odd behavior of her father—the way he had snapped at her inquiries, his sudden preoccupation with business matters he never used to conceal.

Her eyes moved, almost unconsciously, toward the direction of her father's study, with that locked drawer. Last night, she had discovered where he kept the key. The sight of it dangling on his watch chain had become an irritant in her mind, a puzzle she could not solve. But was it really the key itself or what it represented—the secrets he now kept from her—that gnawed at her so persistently?

She shook her head, determined not to let her imagination run wild. It was foolish, really, to assume the worst. There could be any number of innocent reasons for his secrecy—important documents, financial matters, private correspondence. Still, she could not shake the feeling that something was amiss, that a change had taken place in her father, subtle but unmistakable.

A gentle knock at the door drew her back to the present. "My lady," Mary's voice called softly from the hall, "Lord Aston wishes me to adivse you that breakfast is ready."

He did? That was as good as an invitation... or a chance to ask about her "engagement" with Roland Hawthorne. "Thank you, Mary," Carmella replied, smoothing her gown and turning from the window. "I'll be down shortly."

As she descended the grand staircase, Carmella took a deep breath, trying to steady her nerves. She found her father already seated at the breakfast table, his expression hidden behind the wide spread of his morning newspaper. Aunt Eleanor, mercifully, was still abed. Without her aunt's sharp gaze and even sharper tongue to contend with, perhaps Carmella could finally speak with her father openly.

"Good morning, Father," she greeted, sliding into her seat opposite him.

"Good morning," he replied curtly, not looking up.

She busied herself with the teapot, watching him carefully. His brow was furrowed, his mouth set in a tight line—signs she had come to recognise as indications of his distraction. "You seem preoccupied," she ventured, keeping her tone light. "Is there something troubling you?"

Lord Aston folded his paper with a deliberate slowness and set it aside. "Nothing of concern," he said finally, though his tone was brusque. "Merely matters of business."

"Business?" Carmella echoed, feigning casual curiosity. "You've never kept business from me before."

Her father's eyes narrowed slightly, and for a moment, she thought she saw a flicker of something—guilt, perhaps, or annoyance. "There are some things," he said quietly, "that are not for you to worry about."

Carmella bit back a retort, forcing a smile instead. "Of course, Father. I only wish to be of help."

He nodded, though his gaze was distant. "Your concern is noted, but unnecessary," he replied, lifting his cup to his lips.

Was he not going to ask her about Hawthorne, then? Why would he bother sending her word of breakfast being ready unless he wished for her to join him to speak about something? Throughout the rest of the meal, Carmella watched him closely, her mind working furiously. His responses were clipped, his demeanor unusually guarded. Whatever was troubling him, he was determined to keep it from her, which only deepened her suspicion that something was indeed wrong.

After breakfast, she lingered near the dining room, her heart beating a little faster as she saw her father make his way toward his study. She followed quietly, her footsteps light on the plush carpet. As he disappeared inside, she edged closer, standing just outside the door, her breath held.

She could hear the faint rustle of papers, the soft click of a drawer opening and closing. She strained to listen, hoping to catch some clue as to what he was hiding. But then she caught herself—what was she doing, skulking outside his study like a common spy? She turned away quickly, her cheeks flushing with shame. This was not the way to find answers. If her father had something to hide, it was his business, not hers.

Yet, as she walked away, her resolve began to crumble. What if this secret concerned her future, her very life? She needed to know, but not like this—not through furtive glances and stolen moments. No, she would have to confront him directly, when the time was right.

With a sigh, Carmella made her way to the drawing room, her mind still buzzing with questions. She settled herself at the pianoforte, her fingers drifting over the keys. She began to play, letting the soft, flowing melody fill the room, trying to lose herself in the music. But even as she played, her thoughts kept returning to the same troubling place—the locked drawer, the hidden key, and the secrets that seemed to linger in every shadow of the house.

Her fingers moved absently over the keys of the pianoforte, playing a soft, melancholic tune. The music was a comfort, a way to calm her restless thoughts. She was lost in the melody when the sound of the butler clearing his throat pulled her back to the present.

"My lady," the butler announced, "Mr Roland Hawthorne is here to see you."

Carmella's fingers stilled on the keys, and her heart sank. The last thing she needed was an unannounced visit from Roland. She turned slowly on the bench, forcing a polite smile. "Show him in, please, Parker," she replied, though she could not quite keep the reluctance from her voice.

Moments later, Roland entered the room, looking every bit the dashing suitor, his eyes alight with anticipation. "Lady Carmella," he greeted warmly, bowing slightly. "I hope I am not intruding?"

Carmella forced a smile. "Not at all, Mr Hawthorne," she replied, though she could feel her frustration building. "What brings you here this morning?"

Roland's smile widened. "I thought I might call on you, see how you were faring. And, of course, to discuss our... future."

Carmella's smile tightened. "Our future?"

"Yes," Roland said smoothly, guiding her towards the drawing room. "Your father and I had a most enlightening conversation recently. He is quite eager to see our engagement formalised soon."

Carmella's heart clenched with frustration. So her father had been behind this visit. "I see," she said carefully. "And what, pray, did my father say?"

"Oh, surely he has told you that he believes it would be most beneficial for both our families," Roland replied, his tone light but his eyes watchful. "He is quite keen on the idea."

Carmella resisted the urge to sigh. "My father is keen on many ideas," she said lightly. "But I am not so easily persuaded."

Roland chuckled, clearly enjoying the verbal sparring. "Indeed, that is one of the things I find most charming about you, Lady Carmella. You are not like other ladies."

Carmella forced another smile, her mind racing. She needed to turn the conversation away from talk of engagement. "Tell me, Mr Hawthorne," she said, changing tack, "have you seen my father about town recently? He has been so busy with business of late that I scarcely see him myself."

Roland's eyes narrowed slightly, sensing her shift in topic but choosing to play along. "As a matter of fact, I have," he said, a hint of curiosity in his voice. "Just the other day, I saw him in the company of Lord William Chesterfield. Do you recall him?"

Carmella's brow furrowed. "Lord Chesterfield? They have not spoken in years—not since their falling out over that business in the colonies."

"Yes, that's the one," Roland said, nodding. "I was surprised myself. They were in deep conversation, and it seemed rather heated. I caught sight of them just outside White's. Your father looked quite displeased, and Lord Chesterfield... well, he seemed intent on making his point."

A prickle of unease crept down Carmella's spine. "I see," she said slowly. "And did my father mention this meeting to you?"

Roland shook his head. "No, he did not. But he seemed quite eager to have done with the meeting."

Carmella lifted her chin, keeping her expression neutral despite the growing concern twisting in her chest. "Thank you for telling me, Mr Hawthorne," she said, trying to keep her tone light. "I am sure it is nothing of importance."

Roland smiled. "Of course. But if you ever wish to discuss anything, Lady Carmella, I am always at your service."

Chapter Seven

THE STREETS OF LONDON were dark and quiet, the usual bustle of the city muted by the late hour. Robert moved swiftly through the narrow alleys, keeping to the shadows, his senses jangling. The informant followed close behind, his footsteps uneven and hesitant. Robert could hear the man's laboured breathing, the fear evident in every hurried breath.

"We need to move quickly," Robert muttered under his breath, glancing over his shoulder. "Keep your head down and stay close."

The informant nodded, his eyes darting nervously from side to side. "Are you sure this is the only way?" he whispered, his voice quaking. "We'll be seen! I don't know if I can make it."

"You can and you will," Robert replied sharply. "We're almost there. Just stay close and stay quiet."

They emerged from the alley onto a narrow street that led to the river docks. The smell of the Thames hung heavy in the air, a mix of brine and the city's grime. Robert spotted his contact, Garrett, waiting beside a small, unassuming boat tied to the dock. Garrett was a man of few words and fewer scruples, but he was dependable, and Robert had used his services before for discreet transports.

"Evening," Garrett grunted as Robert approached, his voice low and gravelly. "This your man?"

Robert nodded. "Aye. We need to get him upriver, to a quieter port. You've got the boat ready?"

Garrett nodded, his expression grim. "Aye, it's ready. But we'll have to move quick. There've been patrols near the river tonight, asking questions."

Robert turned to the informant, who was staring at the boat with wide, frightened eyes. "Get in," Robert ordered. "And keep your head down. Stay quiet, and do exactly as Garrett tells you. Understand?"

The informant hesitated for a moment, then clambered into the boat, his hands trembling. Robert could see the fear in his eyes, but there was no time for reassurance. They needed to get moving.

Garrett pushed the boat away from the dock, the sound of the oars breaking the water's surface echoing in the still night air. Robert watched as they drifted away, the small boat quickly swallowed by the mist rising off the river. He felt a brief sense of relief knowing the informant was on his way out of London, hopefully beyond the reach of the men searching for him.

With the informant safely on his way, Robert turned back towards the city. He had to move quickly—get off the streets and back to his lodgings before anyone spotted him. The mention of the hired men prowling near the river had only heightened his sense of urgency. He moved swiftly through the darkened streets, keeping to the shadows, his senses alert for any signs of movement.

The informant was on his way to safety, but the danger was far from over. There were still too many unknowns—too many loose threads that could unravel everything he'd worked to keep hidden. His thoughts drifted to the boy's mention of Breck—which led him to consider Lieutenant... well, *Commander*, now—Owen North.

North had once been a comrade in the field, a man Robert trusted implicitly. Now, North was stationed at Whitehall, confined to the labyrinth of government offices, his days filled with the bureaucratic side of intelligence work. But his desk job had not diminished his connections. If anything, it had expanded them. North was uniquely positioned to have his ear to the ground on matters that Robert could only speculate about from the outside.

Reaching out to North could provide a wealth of information. He might have insight into who was pulling the strings behind the scenes, who in the War Office was involved, and whether Lord Aston was truly a player or just a pawn. Yet, Robert couldn't shake the feeling of unease. Involving North meant walking a fine line. The lieutenant was loyal to the Crown and bound by duty—what would he do if he learned of Robert's clandestine activities, activities that might not align with official orders?

He needed to weigh his options carefully. North could be an asset, but only if Robert approached him with the right balance of caution and candor. He couldn't afford to reveal too much—especially not now, with so many eyes watching and so much at stake.

For now, he'd keep North in mind as a possible ally, a card to play if the situation demanded it. But he would proceed carefully. Very carefully. There were too many dangers lurking in the shadows, and one misstep could cost him everything.

Robert reached his temporary lodgings and slipped inside quietly, bolting the door behind him. The room was dark and cold, the only light coming from a single candle lit and set on the table. He crossed to the window, glancing out to ensure he hadn't been followed, then settled into the chair by the table, his thoughts tumbling over one another.

The informant was out of London, but the danger was far from over. Someone would notice that he was missing, and then they would come looking for him... and whoever had helped him. And now, with the added complication of Carmella and her father's potential involvement, the situation was becoming more tangled by the day.

He leaned back in his chair, rubbing a hand over his face. He needed a plan—a way to stay ahead of his enemies while getting closer to the truth. And he needed to figure out how to protect Carmella, even if it meant keeping his distance for now.

T HE LIBRARY WAS QUIET, the only sound the soft crackling of the fire in the hearth. Carmella sat by the window, a book open in her lap, but she hadn't turned a page in what felt like an hour. Her mind was elsewhere, lost in a maze of uncertainty and doubt. She stared out at the London streets, shrouded in the mist of early evening, her thoughts drifting back to the unsettling events of the past few days.

Her father's strange behavior, the whispered rumors, and the sense of something lurking just out of sight—it all weighed heavily on her heart. And then there was Robert. That *had* to be him she had seen—always at a distance, always slipping away before she could speak to him. What was he doing in London? Why hadn't he come to see her, to explain himself?

She closed her eyes, trying to steady her thoughts. Memories of Robert flooded back, unbidden—the way he used to encourage her to write, to pursue her own stories and dreams, even when others dismissed her ambitions as mere fanciful notions. He had always seen that part of her heart, the part that longed for more than what society prescribed. He had understood her in a way no one else ever had, not even her father.

A single tear slipped down her cheek, and she quickly brushed it away. She missed him more than she cared to admit—missed his steady presence, his quiet strength. She wished he were here now, wished she could ask his advice, confide in him her fears about her father. She trusted Robert's judgment—she trusted *him*. But he had remained distant, a shadow in the background, and that hurt more than she wanted to acknowledge.

Was there a reason he kept his distance? Was he involved in something he couldn't speak of? Carmella felt a pang of fear at the thought. She didn't want to believe Robert could be entangled in whatever dark affairs seemed to be closing in around her family. But the sight of him, slipping away like a ghost in the night, filled her with doubt. Perhaps he was in danger, too. Perhaps he stayed away to protect her.

She sighed and closed the book in her lap, her hands trembling slightly. She could feel the weight of her emotions pressing down on her, a mix of longing, fear, and frustration. She had always prided herself on her independence, her ability to face whatever came her way with her head held high. But now, for the first time in a long time, she felt utterly lost. She didn't know who to trust, didn't know where to turn.

The thought of seeing Robert again filled her with both hope and dread. She wanted to believe he could help her, that he could shed some light on the darkness that seemed to be enveloping her family. But she couldn't shake the feeling that he was hiding something, that there was more to his presence in London than he let on.

Tears blurred her vision, and she quickly wiped them away, frustrated with herself. How silly, crying over a man she had not seen in two years! But...

Carmella stood and set the book aside, moving to the window. She gazed out into the foggy night, her heart heavy. Robert still owned that piece of her that had been his since the day he first smiled that bashful smile at her. Indeed, she was still as much his as she had ever been. If only he felt the same.

A knock at the door pulled her from her thoughts. She turned as the door opened, and her maid, Jenny, stepped inside, her expression concerned.

"My lady," Jenny said softly, "is everything well?"

Carmella forced a smile, pushing her worries aside. "Yes, Jenny," she replied, her voice steady. "It is, thank you."

Jenny nodded, though she didn't look convinced. "If you need anything, miss, please let me know."

"I will," Carmella assured her. "Thank you, Jenny."

As Jenny left and the door clicked shut behind her, Carmella remained by the window, her gaze unfocused on the fog-laden streets outside. She felt a heaviness in her chest, a mix of confusion and a longing she could not quite name. Her father's behavior, the whispers of secrets he seemed to be hiding, and the distance Robert had kept from her all muddled together in her mind, creating a knot of anxiety she couldn't untangle.

Her thoughts drifted back to Robert—the way he had once encouraged her to write, to embrace her own voice when no one else had. How she wished he were here now, someone she could trust to see through the shadows around her. She wondered why he had kept away, what kept him silent when she needed him most. Was it danger? Or something else? The uncertainty gnawed at her, and for a moment, she let herself imagine his presence, his steady guidance, before reality pulled her back. Alone in the quiet room, she felt the weight of her own solitude.

R OBERT MOVED PURPOSEFULLY THROUGH the dim streets of London, his footsteps echoing softly against the damp cobblestones. The night was quiet, the usual bustle of the city muted by the late hour and the thick fog that cloaked the streets. With the informant now safely on his way north, Robert should have felt a sense of relief. Instead, a growing unease gripped him, his mind racing with the uncertainties that still lay ahead.

He needed to plan his next move with care. There were too many unknowns—too many players in this game whose motives he couldn't yet discern. The recent developments suggested a deeper conspiracy, one that might involve some of the highest circles of power. If Lord Aston was part of it, or worse, a target of it, Robert needed to find out quickly. And that meant he might have to risk a direct encounter with those involved, however dangerous that might be.

As he continued through the mist-laden streets, his thoughts turned back to Carmella. He had seen her at the ball, then again at the garden party, her eyes searching the crowd, her face a picture of concern. He had kept his distance, not wanting to draw her into his world of shadows and secrets. But now, with her father's name intertwined in his suspicions, he might not have a choice. Carmella moved in the circles he needed to access. She could be his key to unraveling the mystery—if only he could bring himself to involve her.

The thought filled him with dread. He had spent the past two years trying to bury his feelings for Carmella, to move on from the pain of their parting. Involving her now, pulling her into this dangerous game, was the last thing he wanted. But what choice did he have?

He stopped by the edge of the park, looking out over the darkened trees. He knew where he needed to go, who he needed to speak to. But he also knew he needed Carmella. She was his only link to her father, his only way to understand what was happening from the inside.

He took a deep breath, feeling the weight of his decision pressing down on him. He didn't want to see her, didn't want to drag her into his world of secrets and shadows. But there was no other way. He had to take the risk.

Pulling out a scrap of paper, he scribbled a quick note: *Lady Carmella, I need to speak with you. It concerns your father. Meet me at our old place, tomorrow just at the end of the fashionable hour. Come alone.* He hesitated for a moment, then signed it simply: *R.*

He folded the note and slipped it into his pocket. The trellis, outside her room... he had climbed it once before, and he would do so again, just to leave that note for her. He could hardly trust anyone else to carry it.

But seeing Carmella again, involving her in this—it could change everything. And he wasn't sure he was ready for that.

Chapter Eight

T HE TAVERN WAS ALREADY bustling with early morning patrons, the low hum of conversation blending with the clatter of mugs and the occasional burst of laughter. Robert pushed through the heavy wooden door and made his way to the bar, where Bill, the tavern keeper, stood polishing a glass. The air was thick with the scent of ale and freshly baked bread, a comforting familiarity in the midst of the chaos.

"Morning, Bill," Robert greeted, his voice steady as he took a seat at the bar.

"Morning, Robert," Bill replied with a nod, setting the glass aside. "What brings you in at this hour? Thought you might still be sleeping off last night's troubles."

Robert gave a small smile, playing along. "Not much time for sleep these days, I'm afraid. Business to attend to."

Bill raised an eyebrow but didn't press. "Aye, business. Seems there's always some of that around these parts. What can I get you?"

"Just a pint," Robert said, sliding a coin across the counter. "And a favour, if you're willing."

Bill filled a mug from the tap, then set it in front of Robert. "Depends on the favour," he replied, his tone friendly but cautious.

Robert took a sip of the ale, then leaned in closer, lowering his voice. "Got a bit of business to attend to," Robert answered. He reached into his coat and pulled out a folded sheet of paper, its edges worn from being handled. "Need to send a letter. Quietly."

Bill raised an eyebrow but nodded. He was used to Robert's cautious ways and didn't ask questions. "You know I can handle that for you. Just leave it with me, and I'll see it gets where it needs to go."

Robert handed over the letter, sealed with plain wax and bearing no mark of his identity. "I'd appreciate that," he said. "Haven't written to my mother since I returned from France over a fortnight ago. Don't want her worrying."

Bill took the letter and tucked it into his apron pocket. "Don't you worry, lad. I'll see it's sent on its way without a hitch. You've got my word."

"Thanks, Bill," Robert replied, glancing around the room to ensure no one was paying them undue attention. "And, as always, keep it between us."

Bill tucked the note and coins into his apron pocket. "You know me. Discretion is my middle name." He leaned forward slightly, his voice dropping. "But you might want to watch your back, Robert. Word around here is there's been some new faces asking questions. Not the friendly sort, either."

Robert's eyes flicked up to meet Bill's. "Who's asking?"

Bill shrugged. "Couldn't say. But they're looking for someone who fits your description, more or less. Thought you ought to know."

Robert gave a tight nod. "Thanks for the warning. I'll be careful."

Bill gave him a knowing look. "You do that. London's no place for a careless man."

Robert finished his ale and stood, casting a casual glance around the room. As he turned to leave, he nearly collided with a tall, broad-shouldered man entering the tavern.

"Well, I'll be buggared," the man exclaimed, a grin spreading across his face. "Robert Daniels! Is that really you?"

Robert stiffened, then relaxed his posture when he recognised the voice. "Lieutenant Harris," he replied, forcing a smile. "Been a long time."

Harris clapped him on the shoulder, his grip firm. "That's just Harris now. Sold my commission when my uncle took me on at the shipping company."

"Ah. And, Joseph?"

Harris laughed. "You know my brother. He's got a pretty dame in every port and claims he has more prize money put away than Nelson ever did. I'll believe it when I see it. What about you? Thought you might've gone off to the Continent or something. What brings you back to London?"

"Just passing through," Robert said lightly. "A bit of private work these days."

"Private work, eh? That sounds like trouble if I ever heard it. You still in the service?"

"Not exactly," Robert replied, keeping his tone neutral. "Discretionary work."

Harris nodded slowly, his expression thoughtful. "Well, whatever you're up to, you still have the shoulders of an ox and the grip of a bear. You ever think of getting into something where no one shoots at you..." Harris fished in his pocket for his card. "There. I could use a trustworthy man. My uncle is retiring soon, and it's more than I can manage alone."

Robert gave a curt nod. "Thank you. I'll keep that in mind. Good to see you, Harris."

"You too, Daniels," Harris said, his grin fading to a more serious expression. "Take care of yourself."

Robert watched as Harris moved toward the bar, greeting a few of the regulars. He couldn't shake the feeling that the encounter hadn't been entirely coincidental. As he turned to leave, his eyes caught sight of two men near the entrance—men who seemed out of place among the usual patrons. They were standing too still, their eyes tracking the room with a watchfulness that set his instincts on edge.

Robert felt a prickle of unease at the back of his neck. Were they watching him? Had Harris's arrival been a ruse to gauge his reaction, or worse, to flush him out? He decided not to take any chances.

He left the tavern, slipping into the crowd outside. He took a circuitous route back toward his lodgings, weaving through side streets and alleys, his senses alert to any sign of pursuit. Every so often, he glanced back, but the men he had seen in the tavern did not appear to be following him. Still, he couldn't shake the feeling that something was amiss.

When he finally reached his lodgings, he paused at the door, listening for any sound that might indicate he had been followed. Satisfied that he was alone, he slipped inside and quickly made his way up the narrow stairs to his room.

He checked his pocket watch and saw that the appointed time for the meeting with Carmella was nearing. He took a few moments to gather what he might need—a hidden knife, some papers, and the small compass he always carried. His mind raced through the possibilities of how the meeting might unfold.

This meeting was a risk—he knew that much. But it was a risk he had to take. If there was any chance of unravelling the conspiracy around Lord Aston, he needed Carmella's insight. And if there was any chance of keeping her safe, he needed her to trust him, even if it meant revealing more than he was comfortable with.

He took a deep breath, steeling himself for what was to come. Then, with a final glance around the room, he stepped back out into the street, heading toward Hyde Park. The path ahead was uncertain, but Robert knew one thing for sure: whatever happened next could change everything.

C ARMELLA'S HANDS TREMBLED AS she adjusted her bonnet in front of the large gilt-framed mirror. Her fingers fumbled with the delicate ribbons, her nerves betraying her usually steady composure. Jenny, her maid, hovered nearby, holding a pair of gloves and watching her mistress with a concerned expression.

"Are you quite well, my lady?" Jenny asked softly, noticing the way Carmella's hands shook as she tied the bow.

"Yes, Jenny, I am quite well," Carmella replied, though her voice lacked its usual confidence. She turned her head slightly to inspect her reflection from another angle. Was it her imagination, or had she lost some of the freshness that Robert once admired? Her complexion seemed paler than she remembered, her eyes darker with worry. Two years had passed since she had last seen him. Would he notice the changes? Would he still see her as he once did?

Her heart fluttered with a mixture of excitement and fear. The note she had found that morning, wedged in the glass pane of her bedroom window, had been brief but unmistakable in its intent. The moment she saw Robert's familiar handwriting, she felt a jolt of disbelief run through her. It really was *him*—she wasn't imagining things. Those glimpses she thought she had seen of him, the shadowy figure at the ball, the fleeting sight of his face at the garden party—she hadn't been mistaken. He was here in London, and he wanted to see her. The shock of it had left her breathless. Why had he returned after all this time? And why now?

She read the note over and over, her mind racing with questions. What did he want? Did he intend to rekindle their past, or was it something else entirely? Her emotions warred within her: joy at the thought of seeing him again, the man she had once loved so deeply, and fear of what this meeting might mean. She knew the risks, the pain that had followed their last encounter, and yet here he was, asking to meet at the old tree in Hyde Park, where they used to leave secret notes for one another. Memories of those days came flooding back, filled with a bittersweet ache. Did he still care for her? Or was he merely seeking her out for some other purpose?

Her nerves were beginning to fray as the appointed time drew near, her thoughts tangled with hope and trepidation. What if he had come to say goodbye for good this time? Or what if he needed something from her? That was, after all, how they had first met. He in need, and too proud to ask for help. Could that be true again? But no, he was in the army now, or had been the last she heard from him. Was it something to do with his duties? She didn't know whether to be elated or terrified. All she knew was that she had to see him, had to find out for herself why Robert Daniels had returned to her life after so long.

"Thank you, Jenny," she said, taking the gloves from her maid and sliding them onto her hands. "Thank you. That will be all."

Jenny nodded and quietly left the room, leaving Carmella alone with her thoughts. She took a deep breath, smoothing the front of her gown, and then made her way downstairs, where she found Aunt Eleanor seated in the drawing room with a book in hand.

"Aunt Eleanor," Carmella began, trying to keep her voice light and casual, "I thought I might take a drive around Hyde Park this afternoon, for some fresh air. I think it would do me good to be out on my own for a little while."

Aunt Eleanor looked up from her book, her eyes brightening. "A capital idea, my dear," she replied with a smile. "But I shall accompany you. The fresh air will do us both some good."

Carmella's heart sank. "I was rather hoping to go alone, Aunt," she said, doing her best to keep the urgency out of her voice. "Just a quiet drive to clear my mind. I have been feeling rather... introspective of late."

Aunt Eleanor gave her a knowing look. "Nonsense, my dear. A young lady should never be out alone, not even in Hyde Park. You know how people talk. And besides, it's far too easy for someone to lose themselves in their thoughts and not pay attention to their surroundings. I insist."

Carmella bit back her frustration, forcing a smile. "Of course, Aunt. You are quite right," she said, though her heart was heavy with disappointment. She had hoped to make her way to the meeting spot without any chaperone, but it seemed fate had other plans.

As the carriage rolled through the busy streets towards Hyde Park, Carmella's anxiety grew with every passing minute. The clip-clop of the horses' hooves seemed maddeningly slow against the cobblestones, each jolt of the carriage a reminder that time was slipping away. She stared out of the window, her eyes scanning the passing crowds, half-expecting to catch a glimpse of Robert's familiar figure amidst the throng. But he was nowhere to be seen. Her mind was racing with every bump of the road, her thoughts a chaotic whirl. What if he was already there, waiting under the old oak tree, checking his watch, wondering if she would come? She could picture him glancing around, his expression growing more concerned with each passing minute.

She bit her lip, feeling a rush of frustration. Why had Aunt Eleanor insisted on coming along? Of all the days, why today? At every turn, there seemed to be some delay—a carriage with a lame horse in the street, blocking their way, a group of ladies walking together, moving too slowly across the path. Each moment felt like an eternity, each obstacle a personal affront. She imagined Robert's face, his brow furrowed in that way it did when he was worried, and her heart twisted. What would he think if she didn't appear? Would he assume she had changed her mind, that she no longer cared? The thought was unbearable.

The fashionable hour was nearly at its end, the sun inching higher in the sky, casting long shadows across the park. With every passing second, her chance to meet him slipped further away. She had envisioned their reunion countless times since receiving his note that morning, imagining what she might say, how she might explain herself after all these years. But now, the reality of their situation was crashing down on her, and the fear of missing this opportunity tightened like a vice around her chest. Her hands gripped the edge of the carriage seat, her knuckles white, as if holding on could somehow stop time from running out.

She had to find a way to slip away, to reach him before it was too late. Her mind raced, desperately searching for a plan, any plan, that would allow her a moment of freedom. She considered leaping from the carriage when Aunt Eleanor wasn't looking, but dismissed the idea as too reckless, too conspicuous. Yet, every minute they wasted driving in circles felt like a betrayal of the promise she had made to herself—to see him, to finally confront the feelings she had buried for so long. The longer they took, the more her frustration grew, a knot of desperation tightening in her chest. She could not, would not, let this chance slip away.

As they neared the park, her eyes caught sight of a small pond where a group of ducks was swimming leisurely in the sun. Inspiration struck. She turned to Aunt Eleanor, her voice pleading.

"Aunt Eleanor, might we stop for a moment by the pond?" she asked. "I should like to sit for a while, just to watch the ducks. It would be a calming distraction, I think."

Aunt Eleanor raised an eyebrow, clearly finding the notion absurd. "Sit by the pond? At this time of day? It's nearly the heat of the afternoon, Carmella. Surely, it would be more sensible to continue our drive or return home."

"Please, Aunt," Carmella persisted, her voice taking on a slightly desperate edge. "Just a moment to myself. I find I could use a bit of quiet, just to clear my thoughts. Perhaps you could make one more circuit around the park? I saw Lady Harrington earlier, I'm sure she would love to catch up with you."

Aunt Eleanor looked sceptical but seemed to soften at her niece's pleading. "Very well," she relented with a sigh. "But just for a moment. And do keep in mind that propriety is paramount, my dear. We mustn't give anyone cause to gossip."

"Of course, Aunt," Carmella agreed, her heart fluttering with relief. As soon as the carriage slowed and set her down by the pond, she offered a grateful smile. "Thank you."

Aunt Eleanor nodded, though her expression remained slightly disapproving. "Do not wander far," she cautioned. "I shall return shortly."

Carmella waited until the carriage was out of sight before she gathered her skirts and began to hurry down the path. She darted between the trees, her breath quickening with every step. She knew she had only a few precious minutes to reach the old oak, the one where she and Robert used to meet in secret.

As she neared the tree, her breath came in ragged gasps. She scanned the area frantically, looking for any sign of him, but saw nothing. Her heart sank. Had she missed him? Had he already left, thinking she wouldn't come?

She reached the tree and pressed her hand against its familiar bark, the rough texture grounding her for a moment. She fought back tears, feeling the weight of disappointment settle over her like a heavy cloak. She had been so close, and yet...

Just as she was about to turn back, defeated, she caught a glimpse of movement from the corner of her eye, and heard her name as if whispered on the breeze. She turned quickly, her heart leaping in her chest.

There he was—stepping out from a cluster of shrubs, his gaze fixed on her. Robert walked towards her with a determined stride, and for a moment, all the world seemed to stand still.

Chapter Nine

ROBERT STEPPED OUT FROM the dense shrubbery, his breath catching as his eyes locked onto her. Carmella stood by the old oak tree, her back to him, her head turning this way and that, searching. The sight of her made his heart lurch. She was even more beautiful than he remembered. The years had done nothing to diminish her, only added a new depth to her beauty—a grace, a maturity that was somehow both familiar and entirely new. The sunlight filtered through the leaves, casting a dappled pattern across her face, her bonnet framing her delicate features.

He swallowed, his mouth suddenly dry. He hadn't expected this—a simple glimpse of her, and he was a young fool again, standing awkwardly by the tree, watching her from a distance, too nervous to speak. He had been prepared to see her, of course. He had rehearsed in his mind what he would say, how he would explain himself. But now, with her standing there, so close and yet so far, all his carefully crafted words evaporated like morning mist. He felt clumsy, his broad shoulders out of place against her elegant form, his rough hands useless at his sides.

For a moment, he simply stood there, rooted to the spot, his heart hammering in his chest. What could he possibly say to her that would make any of this right? How could he explain two long years of silence, the shadows that had kept him away? He took a breath, tried to steady himself, and then, as if compelled by some invisible force, he stepped forward.

"Carmella," he said, his voice barely more than a whisper. Her name felt foreign on his tongue after so long, yet it carried a weight he could scarcely bear.

She turned sharply at the sound of his voice, her eyes widening in shock. For a moment, neither of them moved, the space between them seeming to stretch infinitely. He saw the surprise in her face, the way her lips parted slightly as if to speak, but no words came. He could not read her expression fully—was it joy? Anger? Fear? Perhaps all three. He dared not hope.

"Robert," she finally managed, her voice soft, almost disbelieving. Hearing her say his name again after all these years sent a jolt through him. It was as though time itself had bent and twisted, bringing him back to a place he thought he had lost forever. He wanted to reach out, to touch her, to assure himself that she was real, but he checked himself, his hands clenching at his sides.

"It's... been a long time," she said, and he could see the struggle in her eyes, the emotions she was holding back.

"Yes," he replied, his voice rougher than he intended. He cleared his throat, trying to find the right words, but they eluded him. She was so close, yet he felt a chasm between them, a gulf created by time and silence and everything that had been left unsaid.

He saw her eyes flicker over his face, her brow furrowing slightly. Was she disappointed in what she saw? Did she see the weariness etched into his features, the scars, both visible and hidden, that he carried from the years apart? He suddenly felt acutely aware of his appearance—his rough clothes, his unshaven face, the way he seemed to take up too much space beside her slender, elegant frame.

"I didn't know if you would come," he said, finally breaking the silence that stretched between them. His voice sounded strange to his own ears, as though it belonged to someone else.

Her lips curved into a faint smile, though he could see the tension behind it. "Neither did I," she confessed. "I wasn't sure if... if I should."

He felt a pang at her words, a sharp reminder of the pain he had caused her. "I know I have no right to ask anything of you, Carmella. Not after the way I left... not after everything."

She looked at him then, truly looked at him, and he felt the weight of her gaze as if it were a physical thing. He could see the questions in her eyes, the hurt, the uncertainty. He wanted to tell her everything, to pour out all the secrets he had kept locked inside, but he knew he couldn't. Not yet. Not here.

"Why now, Robert?" she asked, her voice steady but filled with a vulnerability that cut through him. "Why, after all this time?"

He took a deep breath, feeling the cool air fill his lungs. He had to be careful with his words, had to choose them wisely. "I need your help," he said finally, his voice firm. "Your father... he's involved in something dangerous. Something that could put you both at risk."

Her eyes widened, a flicker of fear crossing her face. "My father? What are you talking about?"

"I don't know everything yet," he admitted, taking a step closer. "But I've been watching him, trying to piece together a puzzle that seems to keep growing. I think he's caught up in something bigger than he realises. Something that could bring harm to him and those around him. I wouldn't have come to you if I didn't believe it was serious."

She hesitated, her gaze shifting away, her expression troubled. He could see the turmoil in her, the battle between her loyalty to her father and the lingering feelings she might still have for him. "And you think I can help?" she asked, her voice quieter now, almost unsure.

"Yes," he said, taking another step closer, his eyes never leaving hers. "You move in circles I can't reach. You hear things, see things that I never could. If we're going to uncover the truth, I need you to trust me, Carmella. Just this once."

She looked at him again, and he felt a flicker of hope. But then her eyes hardened, her shoulders straightening as if bracing against a blow. "And why should I trust you, Robert?" she asked, her voice sharper, the pain clear in her words. "After everything... after you left... why should I believe you now?"

Her words hit him like a physical blow, and he took a step back, the familiar ache of regret settling in his chest. "Because I've never stopped caring," he said, his voice raw with emotion. "Because I would never put you in harm's way unless I truly believed it was the only way to protect you, to protect those you love. I know I've made mistakes. I know I've hurt you. But I need you to trust me now."

The silence stretched again, thick and heavy with all the things they couldn't say. He watched her, his heart in his throat, waiting for her response, hoping against hope that she would find it in herself to believe him, just this once.

She stood there, her expression a mix of fear, anger, and something else he couldn't quite decipher. He could see her weighing her options, her mind racing with all the possibilities. For a moment, he thought she might turn and walk away, leave him standing there with nothing but his regrets. But then she took a deep breath, her lips parting as if to speak.

CARMELLA STOOD FROZEN FOR a moment, Robert's words hanging in the air between them like a heavy mist. She could hardly believe he was here, close enough to touch. The man she had loved so fiercely—the man who had left when she needed him most—was now asking for her trust, her help. The wind rustled the leaves above them, a soft whispering sound that seemed to echo her own confusion.

She studied his face, searching for any hint of deception or regret. He looked older, more rugged, with lines etched around his eyes and mouth that hadn't been there before. Yet his eyes were the same, those deep, blue eyes that had once looked at her with such tenderness. She felt a rush of memories flood over her—the secret notes they used to leave for each other in this very tree, the stolen moments they had shared in her father's garden. Her heart ached with the bittersweet familiarity of it all.

But then the pain came rushing back, too—the hurt, the emptiness of his absence. He hadn't betrayed her, not exactly. He had left because her father had made it clear that a man of Robert's station would never be good enough for her. She had wanted him to stay, to fight for them, to find some way to prove himself. But he had chosen to go, believing the army was his only path to honour, to something more than the life he had known. She had waited for him, hoped he would find a way back to her, but instead, he had disappeared into the fog of war, leaving her with nothing but unanswered questions.

"What do you expect me to say, Robert?" she asked, her voice trembling despite her best efforts to keep it steady. "That I understand why you left? That I'm willing to put it all behind us and pretend like nothing happened?"

She saw a flicker of pain cross his face, and for a moment, she felt a stab of guilt. But she couldn't let herself be swayed by his presence, not this time. Too much was at stake—her heart, her pride, the life she had built without him. She couldn't let herself be drawn back into his orbit without understanding why he had come back.

"Carmella, I didn't leave because I wanted to," Robert said, his voice low, almost pleading. "Your father gave me no choice. I thought if I went away, if I made something of myself, then maybe... maybe I could come back for you, offer you something better. But I never stopped thinking about you. Not for a moment."

She felt a twist of fear at his words, mingled with a flicker of hope. "And now? You've come back because you think you've made something of yourself?" she asked, her tone sharp with the confusion and hurt she still felt. "Or because you think I still care?"

Robert hesitated, and she could see the conflict in his eyes. He wanted to tell her everything; she could sense that, but something was holding him back. "I told you. I've come back because I believe your father is in danger," he said finally. "He's caught up in something bigger than he realises."

Carmella narrowed her eyes until her gaze was focused on a bit of the tree bark—because she couldn't bear to look him in the eye and let him see everything. Her father had been acting strangely lately, it was true. But could she really believe Robert, after everything?

"And you expect me to just... trust you?" she asked, her voice tight with emotion. "After all this time, after you left without a word... why should I believe anything you say?"

She saw his jaw tighten, a muscle working in his cheek. "Because I never stopped caring about you," he said quietly, his gaze locking onto hers. "And because I would never lie to you, not about something like this. I'm not asking you to forgive me, Carmella. I'm asking you to help me, to help your father."

Her heart pounded in her chest, her emotions a storm of confusion and longing. She wanted to believe him, wanted to trust the man she had once loved more than anything. But could she? Could she open herself up to that kind of uncertainty again? She felt tears prickling at the corners of her eyes, and she blinked them back, refusing to let them fall.

She glanced over her shoulder, suddenly remembering where she was. The park was growing quieter, the sun dipping lower in the sky, casting long shadows across the ground. Her aunt would be returning soon, expecting to see her by the duck pond. She had so little time, and so much she needed to understand.

"I don't know if I can trust you, Robert," she said, her voice barely more than a whisper. "But if what you're saying is true... if my father is in danger... I have to do something. I can't just stand by."

Robert nodded, his expression earnest. "That's all I ask. Just... give me a chance to prove to you that I'm telling the truth. Let me show you what I've found. Please, Carmella."

She hesitated, her mind a whirl of indecision. She could feel the seconds ticking by, could almost hear the sound of the carriage wheels approaching. She knew she had to make a decision, had to choose whether to trust him or to walk away. But the thought of losing him again, of letting him slip away without knowing the truth, was too much to bear.

"Then, yes," she said finally, her voice trembling. "I'll help you. But this doesn't mean I've forgiven you, Robert. And it doesn't mean I trust you. It just means... I can't turn my back on my father."

He nodded, a look of relief washing over his face. "Thank you," he said softly. "I promise, you have nothing to fear from me. I'll..." His Adam's apple bobbed visibly. "I'll keep my distance. I don't want to disrupt your life. But I couldn't let anything happen to you."

She gave a small, tight nod, still unsure if she was making the right choice. "We don't have much time," she said, glancing again over her shoulder. "My aunt will be back soon."

"I understand. We'll find a way to meet again to discuss this further. I'll be in touch."

Carmella nodded, her heart still racing. She turned to leave, but then stopped, glancing back at him one last time. "Robert... be careful," she said softly. "Whatever you're involved in... just be careful."

He gave her a faint smile, a shadow of the old Robert she remembered, but there was a sadness in his eyes, a weight that hadn't been there before. "I always am."

Chapter Ten

ROBERT LEFT THE PARK, weaving through the thinning crowd with his thoughts in a tangle. The encounter with Carmella had shaken him in ways he hadn't expected. Seeing her again after so long had brought everything back—the longing, the regret, the sharp sting of choices made and paths taken. He had promised not to interfere in her life, not to expect to reclaim what they once had, but how the devil was he to do that when his heart seized at the mere sight of her? He had seen the flicker of something in her eyes, too—a mix of pain and unspoken questions, and it had cut through him more deeply than he cared to admit.

He walked without direction, his feet moving automatically over the familiar cobblestones. Her voice still echoed in his mind, every word she'd spoken laden with the hurt of his abandonment and the uncertainty of his sudden return. She had bewitched him all over again, without even seeming to wish to do so.

Perhaps it was only his memories of their time together that bound him to her. The way she used to laugh, the way her eyes would light up when she spoke of her dreams. She had been his anchor in a world that often felt chaotic and unforgiving. And yet, when it had mattered most, he had left her—convinced that his departure was the only way to keep her safe, to allow her a chance at a life unburdened by his reputation and the scandal that followed him like a shadow. He had thought it was the right thing to do. But seeing her today, hearing the pain in her voice, he wondered if he had been a fool.

And again, he had promised to keep her safe, without any idea of how he was going to do it. Every step away from Hyde Park felt like a betrayal of that promise, of the fragile trust they had tried to rebuild in their brief exchange. He had told her he wouldn't try to reclaim what they once had, that he would keep his distance. But his heart rebelled against his reason, aching with a longing that felt both reckless and irresistible. How could he protect her, truly, without being near her? Without knowing what dangers lurked in the shadows around her father, around her?

He stopped by the railing overlooking the Serpentine, the water reflecting the darkening sky. A chill breeze rippled across the surface, sending a shiver through him, though he wasn't sure if it was from the cold or the dark thoughts plaguing his mind. He wanted to be the man she could rely on, the one who would shield her from harm. But how could he do that without getting close, without risking everything? The conflict tore at him, the promise he had made, and the desire he couldn't quite bury.

He needed to think, needed to find a way forward that wouldn't put her in more danger than she already was. Lord Aston was involved in something dangerous, of that, he was certain. But the exact nature of it—the players, the motives, the stakes—remained elusive, like shadows just out of reach. He needed more information, needed to understand the game he was walking into.

As he stood there, watching the ripples spread across the water, a thought began to form. He needed a plan, a strategy that didn't rely solely on Carmella's help. He needed someone who knew how to find the right connections and could offer the sort of guidance that Captain Hunt, now retired, could no longer provide.

Owen North. The name resurfaced in his mind like a shard of glass glinting against cobblestones. North had always been resourceful, had contacts that stretched from the dark alleys of London to the polished halls of Whitehall. If anyone could help him learn what he needed, it would be North.

But was it wise to bring North into this? To reveal just how deep he was already in? What if his past with Carmella came to light? For his part, he felt he could trust North, but would she feel betrayed—particularly if North discovered that her father truly was a traitor to the crown? Oh, she would never forgive him for destroying her family!

But he couldn't do this alone, not anymore. Not if there was a credible threat to her safety. North had always been a steady hand, a reliable ally. If he could convince him of the seriousness of the situation, perhaps they could learn what was needed, and perhaps save Aston from himself.

Decision made, Robert pushed away from the railing and began to walk with purpose. He knew where Commander North lived and where he'd be finishing his day at Whitehall. North was revelling in married life, a life away from the risks and danger of underground work. The man who once took an entire squadron of French soldiers into captivity by trickery and surprise was now nothing if not predictable.

He'd spend his days at Whitehall, buried in paperwork, and then take the same route home each evening in his carriage. Robert's plan was risky—after all, North could not be seen as consorting with shady characters—but he was accustomed to taking risks. He just needed a moment with North, a few precious minutes to talk without prying eyes or ears.

Reaching the narrow alley behind Whitehall, Robert positioned himself behind a row of barrels, watching the entrance closely. It wasn't long before he saw North's carriage pull up, the coachman waiting patiently for his master's return. Robert slipped into the shadows, his eyes scanning the street for any signs of unwanted attention. The city moved around him, the ordinary business of the day continuing uninterrupted.

Robert waited in the shadows, his gaze fixed on the entrance of Whitehall. He knew Owen North's new habits well—punctual, predictable, and always the last to leave. The trick would be to catch him off guard, but not so much that he would draw his pistol out of reflex. Robert had been shot at enough by foes. No need to go looking for the same from a friend.

As expected, North emerged from the building, his coat buttoned against the evening chill, a stack of papers clutched in one hand. The carriage was waiting, its driver standing to attention, holding the door open. Robert kept to the shadows, watching carefully as North approached. Just as North stepped into the carriage, Robert moved quickly, crossing the distance in a few long strides.

Before North could settle himself inside, Robert grabbed the edge of the open door and slipped in behind him, closing it softly. The carriage's interior was dim, and the sudden appearance of another figure startled North.

"What the devil?" North snapped, half turning in his seat, his hand instinctively moving toward his coat pocket, where Robert knew he kept a small pistol.

"Easy, North," Robert said in a low voice, raising a hand to show he meant no harm. "Just needed a word, and this seemed like the best way to get it."

"Daniels?"

"Last I checked."

North's eyes narrowed, his posture tense. "In my carriage? You've got a nerve, sneaking up like that. Trying to get yourself shot, are you?"

Robert allowed himself a small, wry smile. "If you'd been paying attention, you'd have seen me coming. I'd say you're getting complacent, sitting behind that desk all day."

North's frown deepened, but his hand moved away from the pistol. "What in blazes do you want, Robert? You know this isn't the place for a chat."

Robert nodded, his expression serious. "I know. But it's urgent. I've uncovered something—something big. I need your help."

North glanced out the window, ensuring no one was watching the carriage, then back at Robert. "Talk quickly, then."

Robert leaned in slightly, his voice low and urgent. "There's something going on with Lord Aston," Robert said urgently. "I was in France recently, and I got a tip—a name dropped that caught my attention. Aston's involved in something dangerous, something that smells like blackmail. I don't have all the details, but I need to know if you've heard anything at Whitehall that might connect to this."

"Lord Aston, as in Chairman of the Committee of Naval Affairs, *that* Lord Aston?"

"I did not know which committees he was on, but yes, the very same. And that makes sense."

North blew out a breath. "And you think he is... what, exactly?"

"I do not know. That is the problem. But I have heard implications of diverting funding, leaking information, and even taking cues from the enemy on plans."

North's brow furrowed. "Those are heavy accusations, Robert. If Aston's involved, you're stepping into some very dark waters."

"I know the risks. But I can't back out now. I need to know who's pulling the strings, and I think Breck's the key. You used to work with him. Can you help me find him?"

North let out a slow breath, glancing at the stack of papers in his hand before meeting Robert's gaze again. "Very well, but you'd better be sure about this. If you're wrong, we are both in hot water."

Robert nodded again. "I understand. But I have no choice. Not with Carmella's safety on the line."

North's eyebrows shot up in surprise. "Carmella?" he repeated, his voice carrying a note of incredulity. "You mean to tell me that all this—" he gestured vaguely around them, "—is about a woman?"

Robert hesitated for a moment, his jaw tightening. He hadn't intended to bring Carmella into this, and he hadn't wanted to expose her to any more danger than necessary. But he could see the scepticism in North's eyes, the doubt that lingered, and he knew he needed to make him understand. "Not just any woman," he said quietly. "Lady Carmella Neville... Lord Aston's daughter."

North blinked, the surprise evident on his face. For a moment, he simply stared at Robert, processing this new information. Then, slowly, a smile began to tug at the corners of his mouth. "So, that's it, then?" he said, a chuckle escaping his lips. "All the time I've known you, I wondered what kept you going, what the meaning was of all those letters... odd looks. I always figured there was some girl back home, but a Lady of rank? That, I didn't see coming."

Robert's face remained serious, but there was a faint hint of colour in his cheeks. "It's more complicated than that," he muttered. "We were... close, once. Before I left to join up. She did write to me for some while, but eventually I quit replying. I thought I was doing the right thing by staying away, by letting her live the life she deserved. But now... now I don't know."

North's amusement faded, his expression softening into something more understanding. "Ah, I see," he said softly. "You've got it bad, haven't you?" He leaned back in his seat, studying Robert with a keen eye. "You know, Daniels, I always knew there was more to you than just the tough soldier act. But an earl's daughter? You never do anything by halves, do you?"

Robert allowed himself a small, wry smile. "I suppose not," he admitted. "But this isn't just about me. If Aston's mixed up in something dangerous, it could blow back on her. And I can't... I can't let that happen. Not to her."

North nodded, his smile fading into a more serious expression. "Very well, Robert," he said quietly. "I'll help you. For her sake. But you'd better be sure about this, because if we're wrong..."

"We won't be," Robert cut in firmly.

North studied him for a moment longer, then nodded. "Very well. Let's find out what's really going on, then."

North reached into his coat and pulled out a small piece of paper, scribbling an address. "This is the last place Breck was seen. Start there. And Robert," he added, his tone serious, "watch your back. You're not invincible."

Robert took the paper, tucking it securely into his coat pocket. "Thanks, North. I owe you one."

North nodded curtly, signalling to the driver to start moving. "Just don't make me regret this, Daniels."

With a final nod, Robert pushed the carriage door open and stepped out before it could gain speed. He landed lightly on the cobblestone street and quickly disappeared into the shadows, his mind already focused on the next steps. He had a lead, a direction, and now, he just needed the courage to see it through.

ROBERT SLIPPED OUT OF the carriage just before it reached North's residence, landing silently on the cobblestone street. He watched the carriage continue down the road, carrying North home, his silhouette fading into the evening mist. The night was cool, the air crisp against his skin, but Robert hardly felt it. His thoughts were consumed by the conversation he had just had, and the uncertainty that seemed to loom over every step he took.

North had given him valuable information, but with it came a warning—a reminder of just how tricky this situation had become. This was not a woodland chase with men who traded ale for secrets. This was London's *ton*—the elite, the powerful, the men who made decisions that swayed an empire. He was nothing more than a former blacksmith who swore an oath to the king. And somehow, *he* was the one who had to make sure a good and innocent lady was not swallowed up by her father's ambition.

Unfortunate lady, to have to rely on him to be her hero.

Robert moved swiftly through the narrow streets, his footsteps echoing softly against the brick walls of the buildings. He turned a corner and made his way toward the small tea shop known for its discretion—a place where secrets were whispered and questions were never asked. It was tucked away in a quiet alley frequented by those who preferred their dealings to go unnoticed. As he approached, he kept his eyes sharp, scanning the street for any signs of trouble. The shop was nearly empty, with just a few patrons scattered at tables, speaking in hushed tones. He slipped inside, choosing a seat in a dark corner where he could watch the entrance.

He ordered a cup of tea, his hand steady as he placed a few coins on the table. His thoughts were still tangled with the image of Carmella—the surprise in her eyes, the unresolved ache of loss between them. But he had to focus on the task at hand. There would be time to sort through his feelings later, if they managed to make it through this ordeal unscathed.

As he waited, his gaze drifted to a familiar figure moving toward him—Balfour. Robert had known Balfour back in his regiment days, a man who always had a finger on the pulse of London's underbelly. Balfour slipped into the seat across from him, a sly grin on his face.

"Daniels," he greeted, keeping his voice low. "Still making friends in low places?"

Robert didn't smile. "What do you want, Balfour?"

"I might ask you the same," Balfour replied, leaning back in his chair. "But I've always been the curious sort. Heard you were poking around in places that don't take kindly to being poked. Thought I'd see for myself."

Robert's expression remained guarded. "Why?"

"Maybe I'm here to help," Balfour replied, leaning back. "Heard you were sniffing around about Lord Aston. Thought you might like a bit of information."

Robert shifted slightly. "I'm listening."

Balfour's grin widened. "Lord Aston's been seen with some interesting company lately. Men who know how to make problems disappear."

Robert's eyes narrowed. "And what do you know about these men?"

Balfour leaned in, his voice dropping to a whisper. "Not much, but I know enough to keep my distance. There's talk of debts—gambling, mostly. And then there's a name that keeps coming up. Baron Whitmore. Nasty piece of work, that one. If Aston's mixed up with him, he's in deeper than he can manage."

Robert felt a chill run through him. Baron Whitmore was known for his connections to the underworld, a man who thrived on others' desperation. If Lord Aston was involved with him, it could explain a lot—the reluctance to support the navy, the sudden pressure to make decisions that went against his principles.

"What else?" Robert pressed. "What do you know about Whitmore?"

Balfour shrugged. "Not much more than the next bloke. He's got his hands in a lot of pies, most of them rotten. But if you're looking for him, you'll find him at his estate, holding court with his cronies. Just don't expect him to roll out the welcome mat."

Robert considered this. It was a lead, albeit a dangerous one. But he was running out of options, and time was not on his side. "Thanks, Balfour," he said finally. "I owe you one."

Balfour waved a hand dismissively. "Just remember who your friends are, Daniels. You're playing a dangerous game."

Robert nodded, his mind already turning over the possibilities. As Balfour left the table, Robert drained his tea, slipping a few coins onto the table before standing. He stepped out into the night, pulling his coat tighter around him. The streets were quiet, the city settling into an uneasy calm. He would need to get a message to Carmella, arrange for them to meet near Whitmore's estate. If they could find a way in, perhaps they could uncover the evidence they needed. But first, he would need to find a way past the Baron's defences.

His breath formed small clouds in the cool air as he made his way down the street, his thoughts focused, his purpose clear. He had to protect Carmella, uncover the truth about Lord Aston, and bring those responsible to justice. There was no room for doubt, no time for hesitation. He was in too deep, and the only way out was through.

Chapter Eleven

C ARMELLA STOOD BEFORE THE mirror, adjusting the delicate lace at her sleeves as Jenny, her maid, moved quietly around her, fussing with the soft folds of her gown. She barely noticed the fabric beneath her fingers, her mind still knotted up in her encounter with Robert at Hyde Park. After all this time—more than a year since his letters had stopped coming, more than a year of wondering what had become of him, if he had forgotten her—he had suddenly reappeared, his expression guarded, his words so formal. To see him again, so close and yet so distant, had been a shock. The warmth that had once flowed so naturally between them seemed replaced by something colder, harder. Duty, he had called it. How bitter that word tasted on her tongue now.

"A pity Lady Eleanor had to return to Sussex before the dinner party, my lady," Jenny asked as she smoothed the fabric.

Carmella hardly noticed the maid's words—her gaze was glassy, fixed on nothing. "Yes," she replied dully. "A pity. I understand my cousin is nearing her confinement, and naturally, my aunt wishes to be at hand for that."

"Of course. Will there be many guests this evening, my lady?"

"Sorry?" Carmella blinked, trying to shake off the ache that settled in her chest whenever she thought of Robert's face, his stern, unyielding expression. "Oh. I... I believe so," she replied, her voice a bit distant. "Father mentioned inviting some notable guests, though he was rather vague about the details."

Jenny smiled, seemingly unaware of her mistress's turmoil. "It sounds like a lovely evening, my lady."

"Hmm." Carmella's gaze flickered back to her reflection, but instead of the elegant young lady in her fine gown, she saw a girl she hardly recognised. There was a tension in her eyes that hadn't been there before, a shadow cast by unanswered questions and lingering doubts. Why had Robert truly come back? Was it only his sense of duty that brought him to her now, nothing more? The idea stung. Once, he had made her believe that love could conquer anything, that they might find a way to be together despite the odds. But now... now it seemed he had moved on, hardened his heart against what once was.

She used to visit his mother back in Sussex, after he left to join the army. She never told the woman why, of course. Robert would not have wanted that. But she used to carry a basket to Mrs Daniels every month and just sit and talk with the mother of the man she loved. Comfort her in her son's absence and assure her that someone, at least, in the neighbourhood saw her as a good woman who had fallen on hard times. Not the disgraced widow of a man who shamed his family by taking his own life.

She still saw to it that the baskets were delivered, even when she was in London. But she had not gone personally in... oh, too long to recall. She simply could no longer bring herself to look Mrs Daniels in the eye and not ask about her son. Mrs Daniels was a kind woman, and, to be truthful, Carmella missed their little afternoon chats. Did Robert ever learn of those? If he did, he never mentioned it in his letters... before he stopped writing.

The sound of carriages arriving outside broke her reverie. Carmella turned to Jenny with a small, tight smile. "That will be all, Jenny. Thank you." The maid bobbed a quick curtsey and left the room, leaving Carmella alone with her thoughts once more.

She turned back to the mirror, adjusting the clasp of her necklace, her fingers lingering over the cool metal. It seemed to burn against her skin, a reminder of everything she could not change. Why had her father been so uncharacteristically hasty, arranging this dinner on such short notice? What was he hoping to achieve tonight? His usual confident demeanour had been replaced by a strange nervousness, a guardedness in his eyes she had never seen before. Was he, too, wrestling with some hidden truth, some silent burden he could not share?

And what was her place in all this? Robert had said little about his intentions, about what he needed from her. Only that there was a duty, a responsibility they both had to see this through. She wondered if he still cared, if any of the warmth that had once lit his eyes when he looked at her remained, buried beneath layers of caution and secrecy. She had once thought she knew him better than anyone, but now... she wasn't so sure.

She took a steadying breath, smoothing the folds of her gown with careful hands. If Robert was right, there could be something here tonight—some hint, some clue about her father's dealings. But the thought of doubting her father left her feeling torn, caught between loyalty and suspicion. She trusted Robert, yet she wanted to believe in her father, too. She would need to tread carefully, keep her wits about her.

As Carmella descended the grand staircase, she swept her eyes over the gathering guests in the drawing room. She recognised most of them—family friends, familiar faces from society gatherings—but a few were strangers to her. She noticed a man with a distinguished profile and observant eyes, standing slightly apart from the others. He seemed to be watching her father closely. When her father approached him, there was a slight hesitation in his smile, a formality in his manner that was out of character.

Interesting.

As she made her way through the room, greeting guests with polite smiles and nods, she caught sight of Roland Hawthorne near the far window. He was speaking with a group of young ladies, his easy charm on full display. When he saw her, his face brightened, and he quickly excused himself, making his way over to her.

"Lady Carmella," he greeted with a slight bow. "You look absolutely radiant this evening."

"Thank you, Mr Hawthorne," she replied, her tone polite but cool. She hadn't expected to see him here tonight, and his presence only added to her discomfort. "I did not realise you would be joining us."

"Your father was kind enough to extend an invitation," Roland said, his smile never wavering. "I was delighted to accept. I must say, it's a rather distinguished company this evening. Your father keeps remarkable friends."

Carmella nodded, her eyes flicking back to her father, who was now deep in conversation with the sharp-eyed man. "Yes, it is quite an assembly," she agreed.

Roland followed her gaze, his expression turning curious. "Who is that gentleman your father is speaking with? I don't believe I've seen him before."

Carmella hesitated, then shook her head. "I am not certain. A new acquaintance, perhaps. My father has been... entertaining several new friends lately."

Roland arched an eyebrow, sensing her unease. "Is everything as it should be, Lady Carmella? You seem... distracted."

She forced a smile. "I am quite well, thank you. Just a bit... preoccupied, I suppose." She couldn't very well tell Roland what was truly on her mind. She wasn't even sure herself. "If you'll excuse me, Mr Hawthorne, I must attend to our other guests."

Roland gave a gracious nod. "Of course. I look forward to speaking with you more later."

Carmella turned away, her gaze once again seeking out her father. She watched as he spoke with the stranger, his expression strained. He was trying to appear relaxed, but she could see the tension in the set of his shoulders, the way his hand gripped his glass a bit too tightly. She edged closer, hoping to overhear their conversation without drawing attention to herself.

"...must understand the urgency," the man was saying in a low voice. "The Admiralty requires a firm commitment. Delays are unacceptable."

Her father's response was barely audible, his tone placating. "I assure you, everything is being handled. There is no need for concern."

The man's expression hardened. "You have obligations, Lord Aston. Ones that must be met. Or do I need to remind you of the consequences?"

Carmella's breath caught. Consequences? What obligations was her father under? She leaned in a bit closer, straining to hear more, but her movement must have caught the man's attention. He glanced sharply in her direction, and she quickly averted her gaze, pretending to admire a nearby vase.

The dining room doors opened, and the butler announced that dinner was served. The guests began to move toward the table, and Carmella reluctantly followed. As always, she found herself seated at the far end of the table from her father, who had the sharp-eyed man on his left. Throughout the first course, she observed them closely. Her father seemed to be struggling to maintain his composure, his face a shade paler than usual.

Conversation around the table was strained—polite but lacking its usual warmth. The usual easy banter was replaced by careful words and guarded glances. As the discussion turned to the state of the navy, the man with the hawkish eyes, seated opposite Lord Aston, seized the moment.

"It is in times like these that we discern who truly understands the subtleties of maintaining power," he said, his tone low but edged with an unmistakable insinuation. "Some might argue for bold actions, aggressive expansions, increased support for our naval forces. But wiser heads know that restraint is often the key to maintaining balance. Perhaps... even reducing the navy's influence in certain areas."

Lord Aston's hand trembled slightly as he reached for his wine glass. "Yes, of course, but one must consider all facets," he replied, striving for a tone of nonchalance, though a tremor ran through his voice. "There are... multiple factors to weigh, especially when the stability of the nation is at stake."

Across the table, Lady Pembroke, a staunch supporter of the navy, raised her eyebrows. "Reducing the navy's influence?" she interjected with a sharp tone. "Surely, sir, you jest. Our navy is the very backbone of our empire's security. To reduce its presence would be to invite chaos."

"Lady Pembroke speaks wisely," added Sir Reginald, an older gentleman with a thick mane of white hair and a deep voice that carried authority. "Our enemies respect us because of our might at sea. We weaken that, we weaken the whole empire."

The strange man offered a thin smile, clearly expecting this rebuttal. "Respect, Sir Reginald, is not always won by the show of force. Sometimes, it is achieved by demonstrating prudence, by knowing when to extend a hand rather than a sword."

Another guest, Lord Whitfield, who had been listening intently, leaned forward. "And yet, we must not forget that an unguarded hand can be easily severed," he said, his voice measured but firm. "Especially when dealing with the likes of Bonaparte. A strong navy is not just a show of power, but a deterrent. To reduce it would be to risk emboldening our enemies."

Lord Aston seemed to grow paler with each word, his eyes darting to the man beside him, then back to his wine glass, as if contemplating how much he dared to say. "Yes... yes, indeed," he murmured, his voice lacking its usual confidence. "But, perhaps... there is merit in considering all perspectives. It would be... prudent not to make hasty decisions."

The strange man's gaze flickered to Lord Aston, his smile not quite reaching his eyes. "Precisely, Lord Aston. We must consider the broader picture. Sometimes, fewer ships can mean more... stability in diplomatic terms. The more we flaunt our naval prowess, the more we risk entangling ourselves in unnecessary conflicts."

Lady Pembroke scoffed, her lips curling in disdain. "Unnecessary conflicts? Our navy protects our trade routes, our colonies. Without it, we are nothing but an island, easily overrun. You speak of restraint, sir, but I see it as folly."

The strange man's expression hardened ever so slightly, though his voice remained smooth. "Restraint is not folly, my lady. It is strategy. There is a wisdom in knowing when to conserve resources, when to bide one's time. Not every challenge is best met with force."

Lord Aston's grip on his wine glass tightened, the knuckles of his hand turning white. "Perhaps... perhaps we must tread carefully," he said, almost to himself. "The cost of war... the cost of maintaining such a fleet... it is not a decision to be taken lightly."

"But nor is the cost of leaving ourselves vulnerable!" Sir Reginald's voice boomed across the table, his fist coming down with a heavy thud. "I fought in the American war, I've seen what happens when we are unprepared. To suggest reducing the navy's influence now, when tensions are high, is sheer madness."

A few heads around the table nodded in agreement, but others seemed swayed by the hawkish man's reasoning, their expressions thoughtful.

The strange man gave a slight nod, acknowledging the tension he had stirred. "It is not madness, Sir Reginald. It is a different approach. A more... calculated one. Less bluster, more brains. Perhaps Lord Aston understands this better than most. After all, his insights into diplomacy are well-known."

Lord Aston seemed to shrink under the attention, his shoulders slumping. "I... I merely believe we must consider all options," he said weakly. "The world is changing, and so must we."

As the man spoke, Lord Aston's grip on his glass tightened, his knuckles whitening against the delicate crystal. His face flushed with a mixture of frustration and something deeper, though Carmella could not quite read it. With a sudden, jerky motion, he set the glass down harder than intended, causing the wine to slosh over the rim and spill onto the tablecloth. The dark red stain spread across the white fabric like a wound, drawing startled gasps from the guests.

Carmella rose immediately. "Father," she said softly, moving quickly to his side, concern etched in her features. "Is something wrong?"

Lord Aston glanced up, his eyes shadowed with unease and anger. "It's... it's nothing," he muttered, pulling his hand away from hers with a quick jerk. "Just a small accident. Nothing to worry about." But Carmella could see the tension in his face, the way his fingers still trembled even as he tried to wipe the spilled wine with a napkin.

The servants hurried in to clear the mess, speaking in hushed tones, but the atmosphere had shifted. The air was thick with a tense, uneasy silence. Carmella watched her father closely, sensing that his composure was hanging by a thread. She glanced at the man across the table, who now wore a smug, satisfied expression as if he had just achieved a private victory.

Her mind spun with questions, a surge of fear gripping her. She needed to speak to her father alone, to understand what was happening and why he seemed so shaken. Waiting for a moment when he appeared distracted, she quietly excused herself from the table and slipped into the hallway. After a few minutes, her father emerged, still dabbing his hands with a handkerchief, his expression strained.

"Father," she began in a low voice, stepping toward him. "May I speak with you?"

He looked up, startled, and quickly shoved the handkerchief into his pocket. "Carmella, you should be entertaining our guests. This is hardly the time—"

"What is happening? Why did that man speak to you like that? And why are you so... tense?"

He hesitated, his eyes flicking nervously down the corridor to ensure they were alone. "It's nothing, Carmella," he said, but his voice was tight, lacking its usual authority. "Just... matters of politics, things you needn't concern yourself with. Leave it be."

"Please, Father," she insisted, her voice low but firm. "I need to know what's going on. I heard some of what that man was saying. What obligations was he referring to? What's happening with the Admiralty?"

Lord Aston's face darkened, his eyes flashing with a mix of anger and fear. "You will stay out of this, Carmella," he snapped. "It does not concern you."

"But it does!" she replied, her voice rising despite herself. "I'm your daughter. I can see that something is terribly wrong. You're not yourself. Why won't you tell me?"

"Because it's none of your business!" he barked, his voice echoing through the empty hallway. He glanced around, then lowered his voice. "You will stay out of it, Carmella. Do you hear me? This is not a matter for young ladies to concern themselves with. Go back to the dinner and forget what you heard."

He turned sharply and walked away, leaving Carmella standing alone in the dimly lit corridor. Her heart was pounding, her hands trembling. Fear tightened in her chest, frustration simmering beneath the surface. She had to understand what was going on, to pierce through the layers of secrecy that seemed to surround her father. Turning to head back to the dining room, she almost stumbled into the hawkish man, who had appeared silently behind her, his presence as unsettling as his gaze.

"Lady Carmella," he greeted her, his tone polite and his smile thin but courteous. "I trust you are enjoying the evening, despite the small mishap at dinner?"

Carmella straightened, maintaining a calm exterior even as her heart fluttered with unease. "I am, thank you," she replied evenly. "Though I confess, I am worried for my father. He seemed... unsettled."

The man's smile remained fixed, his eyes glinting with a hint of something unreadable. "Your father is a man of great wisdom, my lady," he said, his voice steady, almost reassuring. "He understands the complexities of his position, and sometimes, the burdens he carries are not for others to bear. I trust you will allow him the space to manage them as he sees fit."

Carmella held his gaze, sensing an undercurrent to his words, something meant for her alone. "Of course," she answered carefully. "But as his daughter, I cannot help but be concerned."

He inclined his head, his expression softening just enough to suggest understanding. "Naturally. A daughter's care is admirable. But remember, some matters are best left to those who have the experience to handle them. Trust that your father knows what he is doing."

With a slight, courteous bow, he stepped back and turned away, leaving Carmella in the hallway, her thoughts spinning with new uncertainties. His words, though civil, felt like a warning. What were these burdens her father was carrying, and why did they seem so dangerous?

Perhaps Robert was right after all. Whatever was happening, she needed to uncover the truth. And she knew just where to start.

Chapter Twelve

T HE LITTLE BELL ABOVE the bookshop door tinkled softly as Robert stepped inside, the scent of aged paper and ink filling his senses. The bookshop was dimly lit, the afternoon light filtering through the high windows, casting long shadows across the rows of neatly arranged books. It was a quiet place, the kind of place where secrets could be kept between pages and whispers could go unheard. He'd chosen it carefully—a safe location where he could speak to Carmella without drawing attention. Still, his pulse quickened as he scanned the room, searching for her familiar figure.

He spotted Carmella almost immediately. She stood by a tall shelf near the back, her fingers brushing the spines of the books as if lost in thought. She hadn't seen him yet, her expression distant, her mind clearly elsewhere. Robert felt a tug at his chest—an instinct to close the distance between them, to speak her name. But he hesitated.

She looked different here, away from the constraints of society and the watchful eyes of her aunt. More herself. More like the Carmella he remembered from long ago, before the world had driven a wedge between them. Her hair caught the light from the window, casting a soft halo around her, and he felt a sudden, unwelcome rush of memories—afternoons in her father's garden, stolen moments beneath the old oak tree, the way she had looked at him when she thought he might be the answer to all her questions.

He cleared his throat softly, just enough to catch her attention. She turned, and for a brief moment, her eyes widened with surprise—was that relief, or something else?—before she composed herself, her expression settling into a polite, practised smile.

"Robert," she said softly, as if speaking any louder would shatter the fragile calm around them. "You came."

"I said I would. I thought this place would be... discreet enough."

She nodded, tucking the book back onto the shelf with a graceful movement. "It is. My companion, Mrs Dunn, believes I'm searching for a new novel. She shouldn't suspect anything, especially... this time of day."

He offered a small nod, keeping his face neutral, though his heart pounded in his chest. "I thought it best to arrive early," he replied. "I wanted to make sure we could speak privately."

She glanced around, noting the empty spaces between the bookshelves and the shop-keeper, who seemed more interested in his own reading than in his customers. "It's a good place for a quiet conversation," she agreed, moving closer to him, her steps cautious, as if testing the waters.

For a moment, they stood there in silence, the weight of their shared history hanging between them. He could feel her eyes on him, searching his face, perhaps looking for something she had lost or hoped to find again. He resisted the urge to reach out, to touch her hand and reassure her, though every fibre of his being wanted to close the gap between them.

"I know things have been... difficult," he began, his voice low, careful. "But I wouldn't have asked you to meet me unless it was important. You said your father's been acting strangely. I need to understand what's happening. Anything you can tell me might help."

Carmella hesitated, her gaze dropping to the floor for a moment as if gathering her thoughts. "Yes, he has been different," she admitted quietly. "More withdrawn, more secretive. He hardly speaks of anything except his work, and even then, he's vague. And there's been this... tension in him. I see it in the way he holds himself, the way he looks at me sometimes, as if he's worried I might see too much."

Robert listened carefully, his mind working through her words, parsing out every detail. "Did anything happen recently that might explain the change?" he asked. "Anything that stood out to you?"

She shook her head, her brow furrowing slightly. "Not at first. But last night at the dinner party, he was different. There was a man there—a guest I didn't recognise, and no one ever actually introduced me to him. He spoke to Father in a way that seemed... off. Almost as if he was trying to intimidate him, but in a way that was polite, like a game."

Robert's jaw tightened, though he kept his voice calm. "Did you hear what they spoke about?"

"Not clearly," Carmella replied. "But it sounded like he was pushing Father to make a decision or perhaps to avoid making one. I couldn't quite tell. But it left my father unsettled. He spilled his wine, something he never does. I could see the fear in his eyes, Robert. It's not like him at all."

Robert nodded, absorbing her words. It all lined up with what he had suspected, what he had begun to piece together. "You said he's been receiving more letters than usual," he prompted. "And he's keeping them locked away?"

She glanced around nervously, then nodded. "Yes. In his study. He never used to keep anything locked away, not from me. But now... it's as if he's hiding something, something he doesn't want anyone to see."

He could see the worry etched on her face, the strain of not knowing what was happening to her father. He wanted to reassure her, to tell her all would be well, but he couldn't lie to her. Not now. "We need to find out what's in those letters," he said gently. "They could hold the answers we're looking for."

Carmella's eyes met his, and he saw a flicker of determination there. "I'll try," she whispered. "But if he's hiding something... it might not be easy."

"I know," Robert replied, his voice soft. "But I trust you. If anyone can get to the truth, it's you."

They stood there, the silence between them heavy with unspoken words. He wanted to say more, to tell her how much he had missed her, how every day away from her had been a battle against his own heart. But he couldn't bring himself to break the fragile peace they had found in that moment.

"Robert," she said suddenly, her voice barely audible, her eyes searching his face, "speaking of letters... why did you stop writing to me?"

The question hung in the air between them, a heavy weight that Robert had dreaded facing. He felt his chest tighten as he searched for the right words, but all that came was the painful truth. "I thought it was the right thing to do," he said finally, his voice low and rough. "I thought... it would be easier for you. Safer."

"Easier?" she echoed, her tone sharpened by disbelief. "Do you think it's been easy? Wondering why you disappeared, why you suddenly stopped caring?"

He flinched at her words, the pain in them cutting deep. "No," he admitted, feeling the weight of her gaze pressing on him. "No, I don't think it's been easy. Not for a moment."

She took a deep breath, her hands clasped tightly in front of her as if to steady herself. "I wrote to you, Robert. For months, I wrote, thinking you might reply, that you might at least explain why you'd gone. I thought... I thought we had something worth fighting for."

He felt a pang of guilt, sharper than any he had known in battle. "We did," he said softly, his voice almost breaking. "We did, Carmella. But your father made it clear that I was... unworthy. That I had no place in your life."

Carmella's eyes glistened with unshed tears, but her voice remained steady. "Since when did you ever care what my father thought?"

Robert hesitated. How could he explain that it wasn't just her father's disapproval? That it was his own sense of inadequacy, his fear that he could never give her the life she deserved? "It wasn't just that," he said finally. "I thought joining the army might prove my worth, might make me a man your father could accept. But then... everything became more complicated. The war, my duties... I thought I was protecting you by staying away."

She shook her head, her frustration evident. "Protecting me? By abandoning me? That's what you thought?"

"I thought..." He ran a hand through his hair, feeling the frustration build within him. "I thought if I stayed away, you'd be free to find someone better. Someone who could give you the life you deserved."

Her expression softened slightly, a hint of understanding in her eyes, though it was tinged with sadness. "Robert," she said quietly, "you were always the one who saw me for who I really am. Not as some lord's daughter, but as... just me. I didn't need you to prove anything. I needed you to be there."

He felt a lump form in his throat, her words striking at the heart of everything he had struggled with for the past two years. "I wanted to be," he confessed, his voice barely a whisper. "Every day I was away, I wanted to come back to you. But I didn't know how."

They stood there in silence for a moment. Robert could see the pain in her eyes, the hurt he had caused. He wished he could take it all back, erase the mistakes he had made, but he knew he couldn't.

"Why are you here now, Robert?" she asked softly, breaking the silence. "Why come back now, after all this time?"

He hesitated, struggling with how much to reveal. "I told you. I came back because I had to," he said finally. "Because I couldn't stay away any longer. And because... there's a lot more at stake now."

She frowned, confusion and concern mingling on her face. "What do you mean? Specifics, Robert. Stop trying to protect me."

He looked around, ensuring no one was within earshot, then leaned in closer. "There are rumors, Carmella. Whispers about debts, about alliances with dangerous men. And then there's Baron Whitmore—a man who deals in matters that could bring ruin to your father and his name. If he's involved with men like Whitmore, he could be in grave danger."

"Baron Whitmore?" she repeated, her brow furrowing. "I've heard of him, but... why would he have anything to do with my father?"

"Control," Robert said simply. "Leverage. Whitmore preys on those who are desperate, who need favours or who are cornered by debts. If your father owes him... he might be forced into actions he wouldn't otherwise take."

Carmella's face paled, and her hand gripped the edge of the shelf for support. "Are you saying my father is being blackmailed?"

"It's a possibility," Robert replied carefully. "One we can't ignore. And if it's true, then whoever is behind this won't stop until they've got what they want, no matter the cost."

"And if it's not true?"

Robert shifted his jaw. "Then he's a traitor. Which... I hope is not true."

She was silent for a moment, digesting his words. Then, a resolve settled into her features. "What can we do?" she asked quietly. "I can't just stand by."

He felt a surge of admiration for her strength, her determination. "I need you to be my eyes and ears," he said gently. "If you can get close to your father, see what you can learn—letters, meetings, anything unusual. And if you hear anything about Whitmore or his associates, you must let me know."

She nodded slowly, her resolve hardening. "I'll do what I can. But you must be careful, too, Robert. If Whitmore is as dangerous as you say, he won't hesitate to come after you."

A faint smile tugged at his lips. "I've faced worse. But I promise I'll be careful."

They stood there in silence once more, the unspoken tension between them stretching like a tightrope. Robert wanted to reach out, to take her hand, to offer her some comfort, but he had no right. Not after everything that had happened between them.

"Robert," she said finally, her voice softer, almost hesitant, "I never stopped caring. Not for a moment."

His breath caught in his throat. "Neither did I," he confessed. "I've never stopped thinking about you, Carmella. Every day... it's been a battle against myself."

She looked at him, her eyes filled with a mix of hope and pain. "Then don't push me away again," she whispered. "Don't make me feel like a stranger to you."

He nodded, his heart heavy with the weight of her words. "I won't," he promised, his voice firm. "I swear it."

They stood there a moment longer, neither willing to break the fragile connection between them. Then, with a slight nod, Carmella turned and began to walk away, her steps light but deliberate. Robert watched her go, feeling the weight of what had just passed between them—a fragile hope, a promise of something more.

CARMELLA CLOSED THE DOOR of her bedroom behind her, leaning back against it for a moment as she tried to steady her racing heart. Seeing Robert again in the bookshop had stirred up so many emotions, emotions she thought she had buried long ago. His presence, his words, the way he still seemed to care for her despite everything—it was all too much. She removed her hat and gloves with trembling hands, her mind spinning with the memory of his intense gaze, the warmth in his voice when he spoke her name.

She had tried to confront him with anger, with the hurt he had caused by disappearing from her life, but instead, she had found herself drawn to him all over again. A part of her hated him for it—hated herself for being so easily swayed. And yet, there was something else too, something she had almost forgotten: a sense of inspiration, a spark of the person she used to be.

The sound of her father's footsteps pacing in his study across the hall pulled her from her thoughts. She could hear the muted thud of his boots on the rug, the occasional creak of the floorboards beneath him. He had been in there before she left to meet Robert, and it looked as if he had not stirred from there while she was out. She had tried knocking once already, but he had dismissed her with a gruff, "Not now, Carmella. I'm busy."

She sighed, frustration bubbling up inside her. It was all too obvious by now that *something* was wrong, something more than just the usual concerns of a man of his station. There was a fear in his eyes lately that she had never seen before, a tremor in his hands when that strange man spoke of reducing the navy's influence. What was he hiding? And why wouldn't he let her in?

Pushing away from the door, she walked over to her desk, her fingers brushing across the scattered papers and books. Her eyes fell on an old leather-bound journal, tucked beneath a stack of letters. It was her old writing journal, the one she had abandoned years ago after her father had deemed her stories a frivolous waste of time. She pulled it out, the leather cool and familiar against her skin.

Opening the journal, she was greeted by her own neat handwriting, the ink faded but still legible. Half-finished stories, sketches of characters and places she had dreamed up—things she had forgotten she ever wrote. She remembered how Robert used to ask about her stories, his eyes lighting up whenever she shared a new idea with him. He had always encouraged her, telling her that she had a gift, that her words had a way of bringing her thoughts to life.

She ran her fingers over the pages, a soft smile tugging at her lips despite herself. She had missed this—missed feeling like she was creating something, like she was more than just a dutiful daughter with no place to speak her mind. Robert had seen that in her, had believed in her, even when her father had not.

Without thinking, she reached for a pen and dipped it into the inkwell, the nib scratching softly against the paper as she began to write. At first, the words came slowly, hesitantly, like a trickle of water from a long-dry spring. But soon, the ideas flowed more freely, the sentences taking shape with a life of their own. She wrote about a young woman who longed for adventure beyond the confines of her father's estate, who dreamed of far-off lands and untold stories waiting to be written.

As she wrote, she felt a familiar warmth spread through her, a sense of purpose she hadn't felt in years. She was more than the expectations placed upon her, more than the restrictions of her birth. She was Carmella Aston, a woman with her own thoughts, her own desires, her own voice. She had nearly forgotten that part of herself, buried beneath the weight of duty and decorum.

The candle on her desk flickered, the flame dancing in the cool draft from the window. She paused, glancing toward the closed door of her father's study. She would find a way to speak to him, to uncover what was troubling him so deeply. But tonight, there was nothing more she could do. She had to bide her time, be patient.

She looked back down at the page, her hand moving almost of its own accord as she continued to write. For now, she could at least reclaim this part of herself, the part Robert had always seen and cherished. She didn't know if she could trust him completely, not after everything that had happened, but she couldn't deny the way he had awakened something inside her.

As the ink flowed across the page, she felt a growing sense of determination. She would not be kept in the dark, not by her father, not by Robert, not by anyone. She would find the truth, whatever it took. She would protect her father, even if he didn't want her to. And she would protect herself, too—find her own path, write her own story.

The candle burned lower, casting long shadows on the walls, and Carmella finally set down her pen. She closed the journal, a small, satisfied smile on her lips. She had found a piece of herself tonight, a piece she wasn't willing to lose again. She stood and walked to the window, staring out into the night, the stars glittering in the inky sky.

Tomorrow, she would find a way into her father's study. She would read those letters. She would uncover the truth. But tonight, she had found something just as important. She had found herself.

Chapter Thirteen

ROBERT STRODE INTO THE bustling marketplace, the early morning crowd already thick with vendors setting up stalls and shoppers haggling over fresh produce. He kept his head low, his hat brim casting a shadow over his face, but his eyes were sharp, scanning for familiar faces. He needed information, and he knew just where to find it.

"Daniels!" A voice called out from a nearby stall. Robert turned, spotting a tall, lanky man with a mop of unruly brown hair leaning casually against a fruit cart. His clothes were worn, but his eyes were keen—an informant Robert had relied on more than once. The man jerked his head to the side, signalling for Robert to follow him.

Robert moved swiftly, falling in step beside the man as they ducked into a narrow alleyway. "What do you have for me, Finch?" Robert asked in a low voice, glancing over his shoulder to ensure they weren't being followed.

Finch pulled a crumpled piece of paper from his coat pocket, passing it discreetly to Robert. "Heard a whisper last night," Finch said, his voice barely above a whisper. "There's a meetin' tonight, over at that fancy club on St. James's Street. Word is, Whitmore will be there, along with a few others—men with deep pockets and deeper secrets."

Robert unfolded the paper, glancing at the hastily scrawled address. "You're sure Whitmore will be there?"

Finch nodded, his expression serious. "As sure as I can be without bein' inside meself. But I'd be careful if I were you. That place is tighter than a drum, and the likes of you and me wouldn't get past the front door."

Robert's lips tightened into a grim line. "I'll manage. Anything else?"

Finch hesitated, glancing around the alleyway. "There's talk," he said slowly. "Talk that Whitmore's got somethin' on Lord Aston. Somethin' big. Might be why Aston's been actin' strange lately."

Robert's eyes narrowed. "What kind of talk?"

Finch shrugged. "Just whispers. But from what I hear, it's enough to make a man like Aston dance to whatever tune Whitmore plays. You didn't hear it from me, but... some say it's got to do with debts. Big ones. Debts that could ruin a man if they ever came to light."

Robert nodded, tucking the paper into his coat. "Thanks, Finch. Keep your ears open, and let me know if you hear anything else."

Finch gave a quick nod, slipping back into the crowd. Robert watched him go, his mind churning with the new information. Debts. That made sense—Whitmore was known for preying on those in desperate situations, offering money at a price too steep to pay. If Aston was caught in his web, it would explain the sudden shift in his stance on naval support.

Robert needed to get into that club tonight. If Whitmore was meeting with men of influence, there was a good chance they would discuss whatever leverage they held over Aston. But Finch was right; the club was known for its exclusivity and tight security. He couldn't just walk in off the street.

He turned and made his way back to the main road, his thoughts racing. He needed a way in, someone who could vouch for him or provide a distraction. As he walked, his eyes caught a familiar figure in the crowd—Lieutenant Harris, now in civilian clothes, looking every bit the respectable gentleman.

An idea began to form in Robert's mind. He quickened his pace, calling out as he approached. "Harris!"

Harris turned, a look of surprise crossing his face. "Daniels! What are you doing here?"

"Looking for a way into a club I have no business being in," Robert replied with a wry grin. "You still have friends in high places, don't you?"

Harris chuckled. "Maybe. What's this about, Daniels? You're not planning on getting yourself thrown out of another establishment, are you?"

"Not if I can help it," Robert said. "I need to get into the club on St. James's Street tonight. There's a meeting I need to hear. Can you get me in?"

Harris raised an eyebrow, but he didn't hesitate. "I can vouch for you. But you'd better be careful. That place is crawling with the sort who'd rather not see a man like you poking around."

"I'll be discreet," Robert assured him. "I just need to hear what's being said."

Harris nodded slowly. "All right. Meet me outside the club at seven. And for heaven's sake, Daniels, try not to get us both killed."

Robert gave a tight smile. "No promises. But thanks, Harris."

They parted ways, and Robert felt a flicker of hope. He had a way in. Now, all he needed was to keep his wits about him and stay one step ahead of Whitmore and his associates. He would find out what they were planning, and he would find a way to protect Carmella and her father.

He glanced at the paper Finch had given him, then slipped it back into his coat. Tonight, he would get his answers. And then, perhaps, he could finally put an end to this madness.

C ARMELLA STOOD AT THE foot of the grand staircase, her ears tuned to the faint sounds echoing through the house. The front door had just closed with a soft thud—her father leaving for his evening engagement. She had overheard him speaking with his valet earlier, something about a meeting with important men. That would keep him occupied for a while, perhaps long enough for her to execute her plan.

She took a deep breath, steadying her nerves. This was her chance. She had waited patiently for an opportunity like this, and now it was here. With a final glance around the empty hallway, she moved swiftly towards her father's study.

The door was closed but not locked. Carmella pushed it open, careful not to make a sound. The room was dimly lit by the last rays of the setting sun streaming through the tall windows. She stepped inside, her footsteps light on the plush carpet. The scent of leather-bound books and pipe tobacco hung in the air, familiar and strangely comforting.

She had always loved this room as a child, often sneaking in to read the books her father kept on the high shelves. But now, it felt different—foreboding, almost. She shook off the feeling and moved towards the large mahogany desk that dominated the centre of the room.

Her eyes scanned the desk, searching for any sign of the letters she had seen before. There were a few papers scattered on the surface, but nothing that looked particularly incriminating. Her gaze shifted to the drawers. She tugged at the top drawer, and it opened easily. Inside, she found a stack of official-looking documents, but they were nothing more than shipping manifests and trade agreements. She closed it quietly, moving to the next drawer. Locked.

Her heart quickened. This had to be it. She reached into her pocket and pulled out a small hairpin. She had seen servants use them to pick locks before, though she had never tried it herself. With a deep breath, she inserted the pin into the lock, wiggling it gently.

For a moment, nothing happened. Then, with a soft click, the drawer slid open. Carmella let out a breath, a small smile of triumph curling her lips. Inside, she found several letters, each one sealed with a heavy wax stamp. Her father's handwriting marked the front of each envelope.

She picked up the first letter, carefully breaking the seal. Her eyes scanned the contents, but it seemed to be nothing more than a routine correspondence about estate matters. She set it aside, moving to the next one. This letter was different. It was addressed to a man named Whitmore—a name she had heard before at the dinner party, mentioned in hushed tones.

Her fingers trembled slightly as she unfolded the letter, her eyes darting across the page. The contents were vague, but the tone was clear: her father was being pressured, pushed to take actions he didn't want to take. Mentions of debts, of obligations that had to be met, of consequences if they were not.

Carmella's heart sank. This was worse than she had imagined. She knew her father had been acting strangely, but she had never considered that he might be in such deep trouble. She had to tell Robert. He would know what to do.

Just as she was about to slip the letter back into the drawer, she heard the sound of footsteps in the hallway. Panic gripped her. She quickly folded the letter, shoving it into her pocket before closing the drawer as quietly as she could.

The door creaked open, and she spun around to see one of the housemaids standing in the doorway, a look of surprise on her face. "Lady Carmella," the maid stammered, "I didn't realise you were in here."

Carmella forced a smile, her heart still pounding in her chest. "I was just... looking for a book," she lied, gesturing vaguely to the shelves. "I thought I might find something to read."

The maid nodded, still looking a bit uncertain. "Shall I bring you a lamp, my lady? It's getting dark."

Carmella shook her head. "No, thank you, Mary. I was just leaving." She moved quickly past the maid, her steps hurried as she exited the study and closed the door behind her.

Once she was safely in the hallway, she let out a shaky breath, her mind racing. She needed to see Robert, to tell him what she had found. Her father was in more danger than either of them had realised, and she couldn't do this alone.

With a new sense of determination, she made her way back to her room, already planning how she would meet him again. She needed answers, and she needed them soon.

R OBERT STOOD OUTSIDE THE private club on St. James's Street, his eyes fixed on the imposing entrance. The soft glow of gas lamps illuminated the cobbled street, casting long shadows that seemed to stretch towards him like fingers. He adjusted his coat, feeling the reassuring weight of the cane in his hand, and took a deep breath.

Harris appeared beside him, a cautious smile on his lips. "Ready?" he asked, his voice low.

Robert nodded. "As ready as I'll ever be."

They approached the entrance together, Harris nodding to the doorman, who eyed Robert with a hint of suspicion before stepping aside. The heavy oak door swung open, and they stepped into the dimly lit foyer, the sound of low conversation and the clink of glasses filling the air.

"Stick close," Harris murmured, leading the way through a maze of richly decorated rooms. The scent of expensive cigars mingled with the faint notes of brandy, creating an atmosphere of exclusivity and power.

Robert followed, his eyes scanning the room for any sign of Whitmore or the men he knew to be involved. He spotted a group of men gathered in a corner, their heads bent close together in deep conversation. Whitmore was among them, his back to Robert, but the others were strangers—men Robert didn't recognise.

Harris gave a slight nod. "There he is," he whispered. "Now what?"

Robert considered his options. He couldn't get too close without drawing attention, but he needed to hear what was being said. "Let's move to the other side," he suggested. "We can get closer without them noticing."

They circled the room, moving past small clusters of men engaged in quiet discussions. Robert kept his head low, his ears tuned to any scrap of conversation that might prove useful. As they approached the far side of the room, he positioned himself behind a large potted plant, just within earshot of Whitmore and his companions.

"... pressing him harder," one of the men was saying, his voice barely above a whisper. "If your man doesn't comply, we'll have no choice but to expose him."

Whitmore's voice followed, smooth and cold. "He will comply. The debts alone will force his hand. And if not, well, there are other means of persuasion."

Robert's grip tightened on his cane. The rumours were true—someone powerful was pressuring Carmella's father into something he clearly did not want to do. But what exactly were they forcing his hand on? And how did they plan to make him comply?

Another man spoke up, his voice measured but with an undercurrent of urgency. "What about his daughter? A man like him, he would do anything to keep her safe. She could be... useful."

Robert's heart lurched. *Carmella.* They were considering using her as a pawn in whatever game they were playing. He leaned forward, straining to catch every word.

A low chuckle came from Whitmore. "Indeed, a daughter can be quite persuasive when in the right hands. If we need leverage, she could be a... compelling asset. But let us not get ahead of ourselves. For now, our focus remains on her father. He knows the consequences of failing to meet his obligations."

Robert's mind raced. This was worse than he'd imagined. Carmella wasn't just caught in the crossfire; she was being drawn into the centre of it. He needed to get her out of

London, and fast. But he couldn't risk tipping off Whitmore or his associates—they were clearly watching her every move.

He nudged Harris. "We need to go. Now."

Harris didn't ask questions. He simply nodded and led the way back toward the entrance. They moved quickly but calmly, not wanting to draw attention. Robert pushed through the door, Harris at his side, and they hurried down the street, blending into the shadows.

"What was that about?" Harris asked.

"Trouble," Robert replied. "And it's only getting worse."

He quickened his pace, his mind already working on his next move. He needed to find Carmella and get her to safety. Whitmore's threats were too real, too immediate. And even if it cost him his own neck, he couldn't let anything happen to her.

Chapter Fourteen

ROBERT CROUCHED IN THE shadows outside Carmella's townhouse, his eyes locked on the flickering light of the lantern by the front door. He shouldn't be here—he knew that. But after what he had overheard at the club, there was no other choice. Carmella was in immediate danger, and he needed to warn her. Every second counted.

He waited, straining to hear any sounds from inside, any sign of movement. The distant clip-clop of a passing carriage faded, leaving only the rustling leaves in the night breeze. He had to move quickly. He picked up a small pebble from the garden path and tossed it lightly at the window above, the one he knew to be hers. It tapped against the glass twice.

After a moment, the curtain shifted, and he saw her face, her eyes widening in surprise. She disappeared briefly before the side door creaked open, and there she was, stepping into the night, her expression both relieved and cautious.

"Robert," she whispered, her voice barely audible. "What are you doing here? It's not safe."

He took her by the arm, guiding her into the deeper shadows away from the house. "I had to see you," he said, urgency tightening his throat. "There's no time to waste. You're in serious danger."

Her eyes searched his face. "What do you mean? What have you learned?"

"Whitmore and his men," Robert explained, keeping his voice low. "They're planning to use you as leverage against your father. They know he'll do anything to protect you."

She inhaled sharply, but then her gaze steadied, defiance flaring up. "And you expect me to just leave? Abandon my father when he needs me most?"

"Yes," he insisted, his grip on her arm tightening just slightly. "At least until we know more. If you stay here, they could use you to force his hand. You need to get out of London."

She pulled back, shaking her head. "I can't, Robert. My father is in over his head with something dangerous. I need to help him. I can't just run away."

He felt a surge of frustration. She was always so stubborn, so unwilling to see reason when she had set her mind on something. "If you stay, you're putting yourself at risk!" he snapped. "Do you think your father wants that?"

Her eyes flashed. "I'm not a child, Robert. I won't run just because things are dangerous."

He hissed a sigh. He should have known she wouldn't be swayed easily. "Very well," he relented, softening his tone. "But promise me you'll be careful. If you find anything—anything at all—you come to me first. Agreed?"

"Well, I did find something. A—a letter, in his desk drawer. He's in debt to someone, Robert, and they're pressuring him."

Robert swallowed. "So, it *is* true. I heard the same thing, but you found proof? Who wrote the letter, could you tell?"

Carmella shook her head. "No, it was not signed, of course. I can try to find it again, look at the seal. There was no time before."

"Only if you can do so without being detected. Do not risk being found out. Promise me, Carmella! Do not even trust the maids. I know you will try to help your father, help me, but neither of us is helped if you get dragged into this and someone decides to start threatening you next."

She nodded, though her expression was more than a little reluctant. "Agreed. But only if you promise to be careful, too. I cannot bear the thought of losing you again."

The warmth of her words settled over him, stirring something deep inside. He reached out, brushing a stray lock of hair from her face, his hand lingering a moment longer than necessary. "I promise," he said quietly. "I won't let anything happen to either of us."

For a moment, they stood close, the world around them fading into the background. He felt the familiar pull towards her, the unspoken connection that had always existed between them. He wanted to say more, to confess everything he had held back for so long, but the sound of a door opening inside the house snapped him back to reality.

"You need to go," she urged. "Before someone sees you."

He nodded, releasing her hand with reluctance. "Stay safe," he said before slipping back into the shadows, moving quickly away from the house.

As he vanished into the night, he couldn't shake the sense of dread settling in his gut. He needed to act fast, to find a way to protect her from the danger closing in around them.

C ARMELLA STOOD BY THE window of her room, her fingers trembling slightly as she clutched the curtain. She watched as Robert disappeared into the shadows of the garden, his form vanishing into the night. Her heart felt heavy, caught in a whirl of emotions—relief that he was there, fear for what he had told her, and a longing she couldn't quite name.

He had always been like this, she thought—so intense, so fiercely protective. It was what had drawn her to him in the first place. But now, his words echoed in her mind, filling her with dread. Whitmore and his men could use her against her father. She shivered at the thought.

She released the curtain and turned away from the window, trying to steady her breathing. She knew she needed to clear her mind, to think clearly. Perhaps some tea would help. She glanced at the clock on the mantel—it was getting late, but she still had time before bed.

Slipping on a shawl, she made her way quietly down the stairs, careful not to disturb Aunt Eleanor or any of the servants. The house was dimly lit, the flicker of the candles casting long shadows on the walls. As she reached the bottom of the staircase, she hesitated, listening for any sound that might betray someone's presence.

The only sound was the faint ticking of the grandfather clock in the hallway. She moved toward the drawing room, hoping to find some comfort in the familiar surroundings. But as she entered, she nearly bumped into the young maid she had seen in her father's study—a new face, one she hadn't seen before this week.

"Oh, pardon me, my lady," the maid said quickly, her eyes darting away as she curtsied.

Carmella gave a polite smile, though something about the girl's demeanour caught her attention. "I don't believe we've actually been introduced," she said softly. "Are you new here?"

The maid nodded, her gaze still lowered. "Yes, my lady. I've just started this week. Mrs Turner asked me to help with the evening duties."

Carmella studied her for a moment, sensing a slight nervousness in her manner. "I see. Well, welcome. What is your name?"

"Mary, my lady," the maid replied.

Carmella nodded. "Thank you, Mary. I was just coming down for some tea. Could you fetch a pot for me, please?"

Mary curtsied again. "Right away, my lady."

As the maid hurried off toward the kitchen, Carmella watched her go, a strange feeling settling in her stomach. She couldn't quite put her finger on it, but there was something... odd about the way the girl had looked at her. She shook her head, chiding herself for being paranoid. Robert's warning had unsettled her more than she realised.

She moved to the fireplace, absently running her fingers along the marble mantelpiece. The house felt different tonight—colder, somehow. She tried to push the thoughts away, telling herself she was being foolish. Still, she couldn't shake the feeling that something was off.

Moments later, Mary returned with a tray, setting it carefully on the low table by the armchair. "Your tea, my lady," she said, stepping back with another curtsey.

"Thank you, Mary," Carmella replied, watching the girl as she left the room. There it was again—that strange look. Almost as if she were... studying her.

Carmella sat down, her mind racing with questions. Could Robert be right? Was there truly someone watching her, waiting for the right moment to strike? She took a sip of the tea, hoping it would calm her nerves, but her hands were still shaking.

As she sat there in the quiet room, her eyes drifted to the door, half-expecting someone to appear. She knew she was being watched, even if she couldn't see who it was. The thought made her skin prickle with unease. She needed to be careful. She needed to stay alert.

She set the teacup down, deciding she wouldn't linger any longer. She would retire to her room and try to get some rest. But as she rose, she couldn't resist one last glance at the doorway. She saw a shadow flicker—a quick movement—before it disappeared again.

Carmella's breath caught. She wasn't alone. And suddenly, Robert's warning felt all too real.

C ARMELLA LAY IN BED, staring at the ceiling, the events of the evening played over and over in her mind. Where was Robert now? She had never seen him so serious, so determined, and it terrified her to think of what dangers he might be facing to protect her and her father.

She turned restlessly, unable to find a comfortable position. The conversation in the drawing room, the new maid's strange behaviour, Robert's sudden reappearance—it was all too much. She felt as if she were teetering on the edge of a precipice, with no idea of what lay below.

Sighing, she sat up and swung her legs over the side of the bed. There was no use trying to sleep now. Not with her mind in such turmoil. She needed to do something, anything, to distract herself. Then, an idea struck her.

The library.

Her father's study had been an obvious start, but the library might also hold secrets, she was sure of it. There had to be more to this than she had already found. Perhaps, if she looked again, she might discover something that could help her understand what was going on.

She slipped out of bed, pulling a shawl around her shoulders to ward off the evening chill. She moved quietly, so as not to wake Mrs Dunn or any of the servants. The house was silent, the only sound the creaking of the floorboards beneath her feet.

As she approached her father's study, her heart began to beat faster. She hesitated at the door, listening for any sounds from within. She knew her father was out—he had gone to his club, or so he had said. But she could never be too careful. After a moment of silence, she pushed the door open and stepped inside.

The library was dark, the curtains drawn. She reached for the small lamp on the mantel and lit it, casting a dim light over the room. She moved quickly to the bookshelf, running her fingers along the spines of the books. There had to be something here, something she had missed before.

As she searched, her hand brushed against a book that felt different from the others—its spine was smoother, almost as if it had been handled more frequently. She pulled it from the shelf and opened it, her eyes scanning the pages. It was a ledger, filled with numbers and figures, dates and amounts. She flipped through the pages, her eyes narrowing as she tried to make sense of the entries.

Debts.

Carmella blinked as her breath left her lungs. Large sums of money, owed to various names she did not recognise. Some of the amounts were crossed out, while others had been circled or annotated in the margins. Her heart sank as she realised the extent of her father's financial troubles. He was in far deeper than she had imagined.

Her fingers trembled as she continued to turn the pages. There were letters, too, tucked into the back of the ledger—correspondence from various individuals, some polite, others less so. One letter, in particular, caught her eye. It was from a man named Whitmore, and as she read it, she felt a chill run down her spine.

The letter was terse, almost threatening in tone. It spoke of missed payments, of consequences if certain obligations were not met. Her father had written back, pleading for more time, promising to secure funds from an unnamed source. She felt a knot tighten in her stomach. This was worse than she had thought. Whitmore was using her father's debts to control him, to force him into doing things against his will.

Suddenly, she heard a noise—a faint creak from the hallway outside the library. She froze, her breath catching in her throat. Tucking some of the most interesting papers into the pocket of her nightgown, she quickly closed the ledger and shoved it back onto the shelf, her heart racing. She extinguished the lamp and slipped behind the heavy curtains, pressing herself against the wall.

The library door creaked open, and she heard footsteps entering the room. She held her breath, peeking through a small gap in the curtain. The figure was cloaked in shadow, but she could just make out the outline of a man—not her father, and not the butler. This one was taller than her father, more imposing, but his movements were deliberate and unhurried. He was not afraid of being discovered.

Carmella's pulse quickened. She recognised him from the dinner party—a friend of Whitmore's, if he could be called a friend. She watched as he reached for the same ledger she had just held, rifling through the papers there. He seemed to know exactly what he was looking for, his hands moving with practised ease.

She bit her lip, trying to stay calm. What was he looking for? And why was he here? She knew she couldn't let him find her, not like this. She needed to find a way to get out of the study without being seen. Who the devil had let the man into the house?

The man seemed to grow frustrated, muttering under his breath as he searched the book. Eventually, he crammed it back on the bookshelf and moved down the row, his eyes scanning the other titles. She prayed he wouldn't notice the bulge she made in the curtains. She could hear her own breathing, each breath loud in the quiet room.

After what felt like an eternity, the man seemed to give up. He turned, glancing around the room one last time before making his way back to the door. Carmella remained frozen in place, her body tense with fear. She waited until she heard the study door close softly behind him, then slowly released the breath she had been holding.

She stayed hidden for a few moments longer, making sure he was really gone, before stepping out from behind the curtain. She felt a rush of adrenaline coursing through her veins. She needed to get back to her room, to hide the letters she had found and figure out what to do next.

Chapter Fifteen

ROBERT LINGERED NEAR THE entrance of a bustling coaching inn, his posture relaxed and unassuming, as if he were merely a passerby pausing to gather his bearings. The inn was alive with activity despite the early hour, the courtyard filled with the sounds of clattering hooves on cobblestones, the snorts and whinnies of horses being fed and watered, and the low hum of men's voices. The tang of horse sweat and leather mingled with the yeasty smell of freshly baked bread wafting from the kitchen, mingling with the sharp bite of tobacco smoke from pipes lit against the morning chill.

He kept his gaze unfocused, eyes drifting over the assortment of vehicles lined up—sleek, well-appointed carriages belonging to the wealthy mingled with rougher, more utilitarian coaches used for deliveries. His ears, however, were finely tuned, catching snippets of conversations among the drivers and grooms as they swapped news and complaints: grousing about the damp chill that seemed to settle into the bones, grumbling over the rutted state of the roads leading into the city, lamenting the miserly tips of their more parsimonious patrons.

He heard the occasional coarse jest, followed by the burst of rough laughter, but one exchange in particular caught his attention. Just a few paces away, two coachmen stood beside a glossy carriage with a familiar crest on the door, the horses still steaming from a hard ride. One of the men—a burly fellow with a ruddy face, wrapped in a heavy wool coat—was scratching his head, his thick Yorkshire accent cutting through the morning chatter as he sought directions.

"Now, I've got to get to Grosvenor Square from here," the burly coachman said, his voice carrying over the din. "Do you know the quickest way? I'm not from these parts, see—brought my master all the way up from Yorkshire for some gathering with the Bexleys, and now I'm supposed to find my way back. Not keen to lose time on a fool's route."

The other, a lean, weather-beaten man who looked as if he'd been navigating London's streets his entire life, leaned back against the stable wall and considered. "Ah, Grosvenor Square? Aye, I know the way. Straight down this road till you hit Berkeley Street, then take a left. Follow that till you see the gardens, and you're there. Who's your master then, to be staying in such fine company?"

The burly coachman chuckled, adjusting his cap. "Captain Hunt, he is. Good man, served in the Peninsula. Up here with his missus for a bit, visiting some friends in town. Not our usual lot, but orders are orders, eh?"

Robert's heart quickened. Hunt was back in London? Staying with the Bexleys in Grosvenor Square... and now, Robert even had the direction. This was even better than the break he had been hoping for. Hunt was the heir of a landed gentleman, and had a few rather sterling connections. He could rub shoulders with earls and barons.

Without waiting to hear more, Robert turned on his heel and made his way swiftly through the cobbled streets toward Grosvenor Square.

It was a long shot, but Robert had few other options. He tracked down the townhouse that matched the coachman's description and now found himself standing before it, his breath visible in the chill morning air. This had to be the place. Hunt wouldn't be staying in London for long, and Robert needed his help—now more than ever.

He raised his hand and knocked, firm but not loud enough to wake the entire street. After a few tense moments, the door opened a crack, revealing a wary servant who eyed Robert with suspicion.

"Yes?" the servant asked, his tone curt.

"Robert Daniels," he said quietly, keeping his voice low but confident. "I'm here to see Captain Hunt. It's urgent."

The servant's eyes narrowed, lingering on Robert's rough appearance, but he didn't close the door. "Wait here," he said before disappearing back into the house.

Robert took a steadying breath, resisting the urge to glance over his shoulder again. He hated waiting, especially when time was of the essence, but there was no helping it now. Every second counted, and every second was an opportunity for something to go wrong.

A few moments later, the door opened again, and Hunt appeared, looking both surprised and concerned. "Daniels," he said in a low voice, motioning for him to step inside. "Come in, before someone sees you."

Robert slipped inside and followed Hunt down a narrow hallway and into a small drawing room. Hunt closed the door behind them, his expression serious. "What brings you here so early? Has something happened?"

Robert took a deep breath, trying to find the right words as he faced Hunt across the small drawing room. "Captain, I need to ask you a favour," he began slowly, his voice low. "I've come across something—information that could be critical. It involves Whitmore and... an earl. I don't know how deep it goes, but I need to get into that world. I need an introduction."

Hunt's eyes narrowed, studying Robert with a keen interest. "An earl, you say? And you think I'm the man to get you close to him?"

Robert nodded. "I know you have connections, Captain. I wouldn't normally ask, but this is important. You once mentioned a favour done for you by a member of the House of Lords. I need to speak to someone like that—someone who's in the thick of these political circles and might have insight into what's going on."

Hunt tilted his head, considering. "You mean Lord Aston," he said finally. "He's the one who helped me out. Bought my commission, helped me get reassigned... twice, in fact."

Robert's eyes widened in shock. "Aston? Lord Aston?" The name seemed to hang heavily in the air between them. "I didn't realise... I mean, I didn't know you had connections to him."

Hunt nodded, a faint smile playing at the corners of his mouth. "Aye, Aston. Bit of an unexpected ally at the time, truth be told. Came about in a rather peculiar way." Hunt leaned back, his expression softening as if recalling a distant memory. "I ran off a man once, prowling around his daughter's window late at night. That alone was but a little thing, but he rather fancied how discreet I was over the affair. That's how I earned his favour."

Robert's heart lurched. He knew instantly whom Hunt was referring to. "That man... that was *me!*" he blurted out before he could stop himself.

Hunt's eyes widened with surprise, then he burst out laughing. "Well, I'll be blighted! You? I never imagined... Of all the men in London, I never would have thought it was you skulking around Lady Carmella's window."

Robert shifted awkwardly, a wry smile touching his lips. "It was a misunderstanding," he said, a hint of gallows humour in his voice. "But if you didn't already know me to be an honourable man, Captain, I'd have to fear you might arrest me right now."

Hunt chuckled, shaking his head. "You're right about that. Any other day, and I'd have had you in irons for sneaking about like a common thief. But given the circumstances..." His voice trailed off, and his expression grew serious again. "You've got yourself in quite a tangle, Daniels. And now you're dragging me into it."

Robert nodded grimly. "It seems that way. I didn't want to involve you, but I'm running out of options. And if Whitmore's got Aston under his thumb... well, we're dealing with something much bigger than either of us. Tell me, is Aston just desperate, or is he dishonest as well?"

Hunt rubbed his chin thoughtfully, weighing his options. "Aston's a man of principle, but he's not above bending the rules when he feels cornered. If Whitmore's forcing his hand, it could explain a lot. But getting information out of an earl... that's not a simple matter. We'll need a way in, something that makes it worth his while to talk."

"That's where I need your help. Aston trusts you. If you could arrange a meeting, or even just put in a word... I don't need much. Just enough to get me in the door."

Hunt sighed, then gave a reluctant nod. "I can try. But you'd better be prepared, Daniels. Aston's not a man to be trifled with, and Whitmore even less so."

Robert smiled, though there was little humour in it. "When have I ever done things the easy way, Captain?"

Hunt chuckled softly. "That's the truth of it. I'm attending a gathering later today where Aston is expected to be. I could speak to him, feel him out. See if he's willing to talk. But we'll need to be careful. If Whitmore or anyone aligned with him catches wind of this, it could put all of us in danger."

"That's why I came to you," Robert said earnestly. "I trust you, Captain."

Hunt gave a small, thoughtful nod. "Very well. I'll see what I can do. But you must be prepared for the possibility that Aston may not want to talk—at least not openly. He might feel cornered, especially if he's compromised."

"Thank you. I appreciate this more than you know."

As they spoke, the door opened quietly, and Mrs Hunt stepped inside, her entrance lightening the charged atmosphere. "Mr Daniels," she greeted with a warm smile. "It has been some time. I trust you are well?"

Robert nodded, returning the smile with a hint of warmth. "Mrs Hunt. I'm managing, thank you."

She glanced between the two men, sensing the weight of their discussion but choosing not to pry. "If you need anything, Nicholas, do let me know," she said simply. Her tone was light but supportive, a reminder of the partnership she shared with her husband.

Hunt rose from his chair, his expression resolute. "Thank you, Bess. For now, just keep your ears open—but I know you well enough to know that you are already. We might need all the help we can get."

She nodded, giving him a small smile before turning back to Robert. "Good luck, Mr Daniels. I hope you find what you're looking for."

Robert inclined his head. "Thank you, Mrs Hunt."

With a final nod, Hunt turned back to Robert. "I'll make contact with Aston and see where he stands. But be ready, Daniels. Things might move quickly once the word is out."

Robert met his gaze with a determined look of his own. "I'm ready, Captain. Just let me know what you find."

THEY HAD ARGUED AGAIN. Carmella's father had been pressuring her to formalise her arrangement with Roland Hawthorne, but how could she agree to anything of that nature now? The very thought of binding herself to a man like Roland, especially after what she had learned from Robert, made her stomach churn. She had withheld any commitment, deflecting her father's demands with vague assurances. Now, he was not speaking to her. The carriage ride had been fraught with silence, each of them locked in their own thoughts, the carriage wheels clattering over the cobblestones like a drumbeat of tension.

As they arrived at the grand townhouse, Carmella's mind was a swirl of conflicting emotions. She stepped out of the carriage, her hand resting lightly on her father's arm, feeling his rigid posture beneath her touch. The grand entrance was filled with the glow of lanterns, the soft strains of music drifting out from the ballroom beyond. Her father kept her close, his eyes scanning the crowd as they made their way inside, his grip on her arm firm, almost possessive.

The foyer was filled with the murmur of polite conversation and the delicate clinking of glasses. The cream of London society was gathered here tonight, each guest dressed to impress, their faces masked with practiced smiles. Carmella glanced around, feeling a sense of disorientation. She was keenly aware of her father's cold demeanour beside her, his silence a constant reminder of their earlier disagreement.

As they moved further into the room, a familiar voice caught her ear. "Lord Aston! Lady Carmella!" called a well-dressed gentleman with a thick moustache and a booming voice. Her father turned, his expression instantly shifting to a polite smile. "Lord Bexley," he greeted, his tone cordial.

"Delighted you could join us," Lord Bexley replied. His gaze shifted to Carmella, his eyes crinkling with a genial smile. "Lady Carmella, you look as radiant as ever. May I introduce you to a dear friend and guest, Captain Hunt?" He gestured to a tall man standing beside him.

Carmella's breath caught in her throat. *Captain Hunt.* She had heard the name before, two years ago when her father had angrily confronted her about Robert's escape. This was the man her father said hushed up the scandal, who had nearly caught Robert that fateful night. Her very skin crawled, as if he were judging her even now.

Hunt inclined his head politely. "Lady Carmella," he said, his voice even. "A pleasure to finally make your acquaintance."

She forced a smile, her heart pounding. "Captain Hunt, the pleasure is mine," she replied. She felt her father's eyes on her, a silent warning to behave herself. The tension between them had not lessened, even in this grand setting.

Her father interjected, his tone clipped. "Carmella, why don't you take a turn about the room? I need to speak with Captain Hunt privately." His words were more a command than a suggestion.

Carmella hesitated, her eyes darting to Hunt, who gave her a brief, understanding nod. "Of course, Father," she murmured, excusing herself. She moved into the crowd, but she kept glancing back. Why had her father introduced her to Hunt? Was this another attempt to control her, to remind her of the consequences of disobedience?

As Carmella moved deeper into the crowded ballroom, she began keeping her eyes downcast, not wishing to attract conversation with anyone. The soft strains of the orchestra and the buzz of laughter around her barely registered as she tried to calm the storm of emotions swirling inside her.

But before she could find a quiet corner to collect her thoughts, a familiar voice cut through the noise, freezing her in place. "Lady Carmella," came the smooth, self-assured tone of Roland Hawthorne. She looked up to find him standing before her, his tall frame looming over her in his dark evening coat, his eyes glinting with a smug satisfaction that made her skin crawl.

Carmella forced a tight smile, but her heart was already sinking. She knew that look in his eyes all too well—the look of a man who believed he had already won. He reached for her hand, his grip firm and possessive, and she suppressed a sigh as she gently pulled her hand free. "Thank you, Mr Hawthorne," she said, keeping her voice polite yet distant. "You are too kind."

But Roland was not so easily dissuaded. His smile remained, but there was a hard edge to it now, a sharpness in his gaze that made her stomach twist. "I was hoping we could speak privately, Carmella," he said, his tone softening but losing none of its insistence. "There are matters we must discuss regarding our future."

Her future. As if he had any right to dictate what that might be. The very thought of it made her want to scream, but she swallowed her frustration, maintaining her composure. She could feel the walls closing in around her, the weight of her father's expectations pressing down like a vise. "I'm afraid now is not the best time, Mr Hawthorne," she said, stepping back, her eyes darting around for an escape. "Perhaps another evening—"

"Nonsense," Roland cut in, his hand shooting out to grasp her arm, his grip tightening just enough to send a jolt of discomfort up her spine. "It will only take a moment."

Carmella's heart pounded in her chest. She felt trapped, like a bird in a cage, her wings clipped by her father's will and Roland's relentless pursuit. She knew she should refuse him outright, make some excuse to escape his grasp, but she could see the determination in his eyes, the arrogance of a man who was used to getting his way. And her father's stern warning echoed in her mind, reminding her of the consequences if she did not comply. She could not cause a scene here, not with so many watching, not with her father so desperately relying on this match to secure his own freedom.

But the idea of being alone with Roland, of hearing him speak as if their future were a foregone conclusion, made her feel faint. She took a steadying breath, lifting her chin as she met his gaze. "Very well," she said quietly, her voice steady despite the turmoil within her. "A moment, then. But no more."

His smile widened, a triumph she found nauseating, and he began to lead her toward a secluded alcove at the edge of the ballroom. As they walked, Carmella's mind raced. She needed to think, to stay calm. She had to find a way out of this—out of all of it.

She glanced around, hoping to spot a friendly face somewhere in the crowd. If only Robert could be invited to something like this! He would surely come to her aid. But of course, he was nowhere to be seen, and she realised with a sinking heart that she was on her own. She would have to face Roland, and whatever words he had planned, alone.

Carmella turned, desperate for an escape, and saw a woman approaching—a striking figure with a pile of dark hair and deep, expressive eyes. The woman's confident stride and the warmth in her gaze caught Carmella's attention, a sharp contrast to the stifling atmosphere around them.

"Lady Carmella, I believe?" the woman said, her voice low and kind amidst the ball-room's noise. "I do not think we have had the pleasure. I am Mrs Elizabeth Hunt. My husband and I are guests of Lord Bexley this evening."

Carmella blinked, taken aback. She had not heard of Mrs Hunt before, nor did she know why the woman seemed familiar, as if there was something she should remember. Still, there was something instantly calming about her presence.

"Mrs Hunt," Carmella replied, managing a polite smile. "It is a pleasure to meet you."

Mrs Hunt offered a gracious nod. "I hope I'm not intruding, my lady, but I was very much hoping to discover a friendly face here this evening." Her eyes flicked briefly to Roland, who seemed less than pleased by the interruption.

Carmella felt a rush of gratitude. "Not at all, Mrs Hunt. I always welcome opportunities to form new friends."

Mrs Hunt offered Roland a polite nod, which he returned with a slight sneer. "I believe my husband wishes to make your acquaintance, Mr Hawthorne," she said, her tone pleasant but firm. "He is presently speaking with Lord Aston over in the blue salon."

Roland hesitated. "Very well," he muttered, giving Carmella a pointed look. "We will continue our conversation later, Lady Carmella."

As Roland moved away, Mrs Hunt turned to Carmella, her expression kind. "I hope I wasn't too forward," she said quietly. "I thought you might welcome a moment's reprieve."

Carmella exhaled a breath, her shoulders relaxing. "Thank you, Mrs Hunt," she said softly. "I was feeling rather overwhelmed."

The lady smiled. "Please, call me Bess. I know the look of a woman who desires an escape from odious company." She leaned closer, her voice dropping to a whisper. "And if I may be so bold, I've heard quite enough about Mr Hawthorne to know he's not the most charming of company."

Carmella couldn't help but laugh softly. "You have no idea how grateful I am to hear you say that."

Bess's eyes twinkled with amusement. "Oh, I think I do. Now, would you like to join me for a walk on the terrace? The air in here is rather stifling, and I find a bit of fresh air does wonders."

Carmella nodded, grateful for the offer. As they stepped out onto the terrace, the cool night air was a welcome contrast to the warmth inside. Mrs Hunt kept up a light conversation, speaking of the countryside and her fondness for quiet, simple pleasures. She was not formed for Society functions, she said—rather, she hinted at the very humblest of origins, but Carmella dared not ask more where every word could be overheard. Still, she found herself relaxing in the woman's company, enjoying the momentary respite from the pressures of the evening.

But Carmella's thoughts were scattered, a jumble of emotions she struggled to suppress. She tried to focus on Mrs Hunt's conversation, but her mind kept wandering. She gazed absently across the terrace, watching the flickering shadows cast by the lanterns.

And then, out of the corner of her eye, she caught a movement. At first, she thought it was a trick of the light, a shifting shadow in the dimness beyond the terrace. But as she looked more closely, her breath caught in her throat.

Robert, dressed in a footman's uniform! He gave her a subtle nod, his eyes filled with urgency. Carmella's heart began to race. She turned to Bess, her voice barely a whisper. "Mrs Hunt, would you mind terribly if I stepped away for a moment? There is someone I need to speak with... privately."

Bess followed her gaze and gave a slight nod of understanding. "Of course. I'll cover for you if anyone asks."

Carmella offered her a grateful smile before slipping away, moving quickly to meet Robert in the shadows. "What are you doing here?" she whispered, glancing around to ensure no one was watching.

"I had to warn you," Robert said, his voice low but intense. "Your father is in deeper than I thought, and Hunt is here to try and help. But it's not safe. I needed to let you know."

Carmella's eyes widened. "Captain Hunt? You *know* him?"

"Yes," Robert replied. "He's a friend, someone I trust. And that lady you were just taking to—aye! The tales I could tell you about her!"

"But Robert, there is something you do not know. That night, at my window—"

He held up a hand. "I know. A rather strange coincidence, but Hunt later became my commanding officer and a man I would give my life in serving. I asked Mrs Hunt to look out for you this evening. She's a sharp one, is Bess Hunt—probably the only lady in that ballroom who would not hesitate to draw a man's sword out of his own scabbard and hold it to his throat. But right now, you need to be careful. Stay close to the others and don't do anything that might draw attention. We're working on a plan, but it's going to take time."

She nodded, her mind racing with the implications of his words. "And my father? What about him?"

"We're trying to find out more," Robert said softly. "But until we know for sure, you need to be cautious. If anything happens, I'll be watching. I'll find you."

Before she could say more, the sound of approaching footsteps forced them apart. Robert disappeared back into the shadows, blending seamlessly with the other footmen, while Carmella returned to the terrace, her heart pounding.

She rejoined Bess Hunt, who gave her a questioning look. "Is everything all right?"

Carmella forced a smile, though her mind was still spinning. "Yes, thank you. Just... a bit of family business."

Bess nodded, her expression sympathetic. "I understand. Family can be quite... complicated."

Carmella only nodded in agreement. The lady might understand precisely what Carmella meant, but the less said, the better.

Chapter Sixteen

As the evening wore on, the strains of the orchestra grew more lively, the clinking of glasses and the soft murmur of voices blending into a heady symphony. Carmella had tried to stay close to Mrs Hunt—the captain's wife was, after all, a willing and rather capable buffer against other conversations she would rather not have. But they could not remain together through the whole of the evening, and so now, Carmella drifted through the crowd, her steps light but her heart heavy. She kept one eye on her father, who stood with a group of men across the room, his posture stiff and his expression tense. He seemed distracted, his usual charm missing, and his smile, when it came, was strained.

She watched as he excused himself from the group, stepping away from the crowd and moving toward a quieter corner of the room, away from prying eyes. He lifted his glass to his lips, his hand trembling ever so slightly. Carmella's heart clenched at the sight. She had to speak with him, to find out what was troubling him so deeply.

Carmella took a deep breath, steeling herself. She scanned the room, searching for Robert, but there was no sign of him. For a brief moment, she considered seeking out Captain Hunt again, but she dismissed the thought. No, this was something she needed to handle herself. She moved quickly, weaving through the throng of guests, her steps purposeful but unhurried, her face a mask of polite calm.

As she reached her father, she touched his arm gently, her voice barely above a whisper. "Father, please," she implored softly, her eyes searching his. "May we speak for a moment? In private?"

Lord Aston stiffened at her touch, his eyes narrowing as he glanced down at her. "Carmella," he muttered, irritation lacing his tone. "This is hardly the time or place for—"

"Please," she pressed, her voice urgent but quiet. She gestured subtly towards a small alcove just beyond the ballroom, where the music would mask their voices. "Just a moment, Father. I beg you."

He hesitated, glancing around to see if anyone was watching, then sighed heavily, nodding. "Very well," he said, his voice strained. "But make it quick."

They moved to the alcove, slipping behind the curtain that shielded them from the view of the other guests. The swell of the music covered their voices, and for a moment, they were in their own world, apart from the glittering ballroom.

Carmella turned to face him, her heart pounding in her chest. "Father, I know about the debts," she began, her voice low but steady. "I know what Whitmore is doing to you. Please, let me help."

Her father's expression shifted immediately, a flash of fear crossing his eyes. He glanced around again, as if ensuring no one could hear. "You do not understand," he hissed, his voice barely a whisper. "This is not your concern, Carmella. Go back to the party."

"But it *is* my concern," she insisted, her grip tightening on his arm. "He is manipulating you, forcing you to—"

"Enough!" Lord Aston snapped, his voice cutting through her words. He looked around again, then took a deep breath, lowering his voice once more. "You have no idea what you are talking about. This is far more complicated than you realise. Whitmore is... dangerous. We cannot simply defy him."

"But there must be something we can do," she whispered fiercely. "We cannot let him control us like this."

He looked at her, his expression softening for a moment. "I am trying to protect you," he said quietly, his voice rough with emotion. "Everything I have done, I have done for you. You must trust me."

She shook her head, her resolve hardening. "I do trust you, Father. But I cannot stand by and watch as you are destroyed by this man. There are people here tonight who want to help—Captain Hunt, perhaps. You must speak with him, let him know—"

Lord Aston's face paled, his eyes widening. "Captain Hunt?" he repeated, a note of fear creeping into his voice. "Why would he... Carmella, have you spoken to him about this?"

"No, not directly," she admitted. "But he knows something is amiss. He could be an ally—"

"No!" her father cut her off sharply. "You must not involve him in this. If Whitmore finds out... if he suspects—"

Carmella frowned, frustration boiling within her. "Then what, Father? What happens then?"

Lord Aston hesitated, his gaze flicking back toward Whitmore, who was still engrossed in conversation across the room. "I cannot say," he muttered. "Just... keep your distance. Do not draw attention to yourself, and do not look as if you mean to defy my wishes."

She narrowed her eyes. "Do you mean..."

"The best way you can appear to be compliant is to take up with Mr Hawthorne. Please, Carmella. You cannot know how many eyes are watching you."

"But I do not trust Hawthorne!" She opened her mouth to argue further, but her father gave her a warning look, his expression taut with fear and something else—perhaps guilt.

"Please, Carmella," he said softly. "Just do as I ask."

She bit her lip, nodding reluctantly. "I... I will, Father," she murmured, though her heart was still heavy with worry. "But promise me you will be careful."

He gave her a faint, weary smile. "I promise," he said quietly. "Now, go. Before anyone notices us."

With a final, lingering glance, Carmella stepped away, returning to the ballroom. She cast a quick look around, her eyes scanning the crowd for Robert. She still couldn't see him, but she felt a flicker of hope—if Captain Hunt was here, then Robert couldn't be far behind.

As she moved back into the throng of guests, she resolved to find Hunt and speak to him herself. She couldn't let this go, not now. Not when her father's future—and possibly her own—hung in the balance.

R OBERT POSITIONED HIMSELF NEAR the edge of the ballroom, keeping to the shadows where the flickering candlelight didn't quite reach. The footman's uniform felt strange on him—too tight across the shoulders, the starched collar stiff against his neck—but it served its purpose. No one paid him any mind. To the finely dressed guests, he was just another servant.

His eyes tracked Carmella as she moved through the crowd, a forced smile on her lips. More often than not, she was on the arm of Roland Hawthorne, and Robert's blood boiled each time the man touched her. She was a vision in her emerald gown, her hair pinned in an elegant twist. But Robert could see the tension in her posture, the way her fingers gripped the stem of her wine glass a bit too tightly. She was worried. She was playing her part, but her eyes kept darting toward her father, who was deep in conversation with Whitmore and another gentleman.

Robert's gaze shifted to Lord Aston. The man looked more drawn than ever, his face pale under the ballroom's bright lights. He nodded absently to whatever Whitmore was saying, but there was a tightness in his expression, a strain that spoke of deeper concerns. Robert knew that look well. It was the look of a man being pushed to his limits.

Suddenly, a burst of laughter drew Robert's attention back to Carmella. Roland Hawthorne had rejoined her, his face flushed with wine and self-satisfaction. He took her hand, lifting it high as if to show her off to the room.

"Ladies and gentlemen," Hawthorne called out, his voice booming over the soft strains of the orchestra. "A moment of your attention, if you please!"

The chatter in the room quieted, and all eyes turned toward them. Robert's heart thudded in his chest. What was Hawthorne playing at?

"I have the great pleasure to announce," Hawthorne continued, "that Lady Carmella and I are to be married!"

A murmur of surprise rippled through the crowd, followed by polite applause. Robert's stomach twisted as he watched Carmella's face. She looked stunned, her eyes wide with shock, and then her expression hardened. She pulled her hand away from Hawthorne's grip, but he held on, smiling broadly as if nothing were amiss.

Robert's fists clenched at his sides, his pulse pounding in his ears. This wasn't Carmella's doing. She wouldn't have agreed to such a thing, not like this, not without a word. He could see the anger in her eyes, the way her chin lifted defiantly.

He had to do something. He couldn't stand by and let Hawthorne trap her in this farce. But what could he do, dressed as a footman, without blowing his cover? He glanced around the room, searching for Hunt. The captain was talking with a few other gentlemen, but Robert caught his eye and gave a quick, subtle signal. Hunt's face registered surprise, but he quickly masked it, giving Robert a barely perceptible nod.

What to do now? He needed to act, but he couldn't be rash. If he moved too soon, he could ruin everything. But if he did nothing... He couldn't bear the thought of Carmella being forced into a marriage with a man like Hawthorne. His jaw tightened. No, he wouldn't let that happen. Not while he still had breath in his body.

He watched as Carmella turned on her heel, moving quickly toward a side door that led to the terrace. Hawthorne, taken aback by her sudden movement, followed her, his expression darkening. Robert saw his chance. He moved swiftly, weaving through the guests, careful not to draw attention.

As he reached the door, he paused just inside the threshold, listening. The cool night air drifted in from the terrace, mingling with the warmth of the ballroom. He could hear their voices outside—Carmella's, sharp with anger, and Hawthorne's, low and cajoling.

"I never agreed to this, Mr Hawthorne!" Carmella's voice trembled with fury. "How dare you make such an announcement without my consent!"

"Come now, my dear," Hawthorne replied smoothly, though there was a hard edge to his tone. "It's only a matter of time. Why not let everyone know of our... impending happiness?"

"There is no happiness in deceit!" Carmella shot back. "Release me this instant!"

Robert's heart clenched at the distress in her voice. He stepped out onto the terrace, his movements quiet, his eyes fixed on the pair. "Is there a problem here, my lady?" he asked, his voice low and steady.

Carmella turned, her eyes widening in relief at the sight of him.

Hawthorne's face darkened with recognition, and he sneered. "And who are you to interfere, servant?"

Robert didn't flinch. "A concerned observer," he replied calmly. "It appears the lady is not entirely pleased with your actions, sir."

Hawthorne's eyes narrowed. "This is none of your concern. Leave us."

But Robert didn't move. "I believe it is my concern if a lady's wishes are being disregarded. And I don't think her father would appreciate his daughter being pressured into something against her will."

Hawthorne's jaw tightened, and for a moment, Robert thought he might lash out. But then Hawthorne seemed to reconsider, glancing back toward the ballroom where Lord Aston stood, watching them with a frown. "Very well," Hawthorne said through gritted teeth, releasing Carmella's arm. "I shall go and speak privately with him now. Will that satisfy you, my dear?" He shot his cuffs and gestured airily to Robert. "Fetch the lady a glass. Two, if you please. We shall drink to our happiness when I return."

Carmella took a step back as Hawthorne left, her breath coming in quick, shallow gasps. Robert moved to her side, offering his arm. "Are you well?" he asked softly, his eyes searching hers.

She nodded, though her face was pale. "Thank you," she whispered. "But we need to talk. There's so much you don't know."

Robert nodded. "I'm here," he said quietly. "I'm not going anywhere. Not this time."

Carmella clung to Robert's arm as he opened the door from the terrace. "Best not to be here when Hawthorne returns," he had said.

Carmella nodded and, only belatedly, realised that she could not be seen hanging on the arm of a "footman." She released him, but he did not go far—walking just behind her, near enough for her to feel the tickle of his breath stirring the hair at her neck. The warmth of his presence was both a comfort and a reminder of how much had changed—and yet, how much had stayed the same.

Robert kept his steps measured as he escorted her back toward the ballroom, careful not to draw any unnecessary attention. His footman's uniform was a clever disguise, but they both knew it wouldn't hold up under scrutiny for long.

"Stay close to the wall," he murmured softly, his voice barely more than a breath against her ear. "I'll find Hunt. He's our best chance now."

She nodded, her breath still coming in shallow gasps, her thoughts whirling with everything she'd learned tonight. "Be careful, Robert," she whispered back. "Whitmore's men are everywhere."

His lips tightened into a grim line. "I know," he said. "But I won't let anything happen to you. I promise."

They reached a quieter corner of the ballroom, just behind a grand pillar that shielded them from the main gathering. Robert glanced around, ensuring they were momentarily alone, then released her arm. "Stay here," he instructed. "I'll be back as soon as I can. And remember, don't draw attention to yourself."

Carmella watched him slip away, blending seamlessly into the shadows. She felt a pang of worry, her gaze lingering on his retreating form. But she knew he was right—they needed more information, and Hunt was the best person to help them. She turned her attention back to the room, forcing herself to appear calm, though her nerves were frayed. She needed to act normally, to not arouse suspicion.

Just as she began to move toward the safety of a nearby group of ladies, she felt a cold, familiar presence close by. She turned, her breath catching in her throat as she saw Roland Hawthorne approaching, a confident smirk playing at his lips. He cut through the crowd with an easy grace, his dark evening coat brushing against the floor.

"Lady Carmella," he greeted her, his voice smooth as he took her hand without waiting for permission. "There you are. I was beginning to think you had slipped away again."

Carmella forced a tight smile, pulling her hand back as discreetly as she could. "Mr Hawthorne," she replied, keeping her tone civil. "I had hoped to avoid further misunderstandings tonight. I am sure you can appreciate that."

Roland's eyes darkened, and he leaned closer, his voice dropping to a low murmur. "I understand perfectly, my dear. And I also understand the importance of appearances. We wouldn't want to cause any scandal now, would we?"

Carmella's heart sank. She knew what he was doing—using the threat of gossip to pressure her. She glanced around, noting the curious glances of nearby guests. "Mr Hawthorne, I have already explained—"

Before she could finish, Roland straightened and turned to address the room, his voice booming with an easy confidence. "Ladies and gentlemen," he called out, a broad grin spreading across his face, "it seems our lovely Lady Carmella is feeling a bit of cold feet this evening. Perhaps she fears that I will whisk her away too quickly from all this fine company!"

A ripple of laughter moved through the crowd, and Carmella felt her cheeks flush with a mix of embarrassment and frustration. Roland's jest, though seemingly harmless, painted her as a reluctant bride-to-be, coyly resisting his advances rather than firmly opposing them.

"Oh, but what a joyous occasion it will be!" Roland continued, clearly enjoying the attention. He gestured grandly with his arm, turning a charming smile on several ladies nearby who watched with amused curiosity. "I assure you, there will be a celebration like no other. Isn't that right, Lady Carmella?"

Carmella's heart pounded in her chest. She knew she needed to speak up, to set the record straight, but every eye in the room was on her, expecting her to play along with the farce. She swallowed hard, trying to gather her courage. "Mr Hawthorne, I—"

But Roland cut her off, his voice smoothly overtaking hers. "Ah, yes, Lady Carmella is simply overwhelmed with joy. It's understandable, of course," he said with a wink, eliciting another round of polite chuckles from the guests.

The laughter felt like needles pricking her skin. She opened her mouth to protest again, but before she could say anything, Robert appeared at her side, dressed in his footman's uniform, his face calm but his eyes sharp with intensity.

"Excuse me, Mr Hawthorne," Robert interjected smoothly, bowing slightly. "The lady has not yet given her consent. I believe it would be proper to let her speak for herself."

A murmur went through the crowd, the laughter dying down as attention shifted to Robert. Roland's smile faltered for a brief moment, a flash of annoyance crossing his features. "And who might you be, footman, to involve yourself in matters above your station?" he demanded, his tone colder now.

Robert maintained his composure, his gaze steady on Roland. "Just a servant of the household, sir," he said calmly. "It would be wise not to force a lady's hand in public, sir. It rarely ends well."

Roland's face flushed with anger. "You have overstepped your bounds, footman," he hissed. "Do you know who I am?"

"I know exactly who you are," Robert answered, his gaze unwavering. "And I know that a true gentleman doesn't make announcements on behalf of a lady without her explicit consent."

The tension between them crackled in the air, drawing the attention of more guests. Roland seemed to realise he was making a scene and forced a tight, condescending smile. "Of course," he said, his tone oily. "I wouldn't dream of imposing on Lady Carmella's will. My apologies if I spoke out of turn."

He turned back to Carmella, his eyes gleaming with a mix of frustration and something darker. "We will speak later," he said quietly, his voice barely masking his anger. "In private."

Carmella nodded, her throat tight. "Yes, of course," she managed, though her heart was still pounding. As Roland moved away, she felt Robert's hand gently guide her away from the crowd toward a quieter corner.

"Are you well?" Robert asked, his voice low and filled with concern. "I'm sorry. I couldn't get back sooner."

Carmella nodded, taking a shaky breath. "Yes, I—thank you, Robert. I didn't know what to do. He just... announced it again without even asking me."

Robert's jaw tightened. "He's desperate. Whitmore's hold on him must be tighter than we thought. We need to get you and your father away from here."

Carmella looked over at her father, still in a tense conversation with Whitmore. "Father... he's in deeper than I realised. I have to help him, Robert. I can't just leave."

Robert's gaze softened, and he nodded. "I'll find Hunt. He might have a way to turn the tables on Whitmore and his men."

She squeezed his hand, her heart aching with gratitude. "Thank you, Robert. For everything."

He gave her a small, reassuring smile. "I'll be back soon. Just stay where it's safe."

He slipped away into the crowd again, his eyes scanning for Hunt. Carmella watched him go, her heart torn between fear for her father and the growing realisation of her own feelings for Robert. She had to trust him—had to believe they could find a way out of this together.

But as she turned back toward her father, she saw Whitmore's eyes locked on her, his expression one of cold calculation.

Chapter Seventeen

"LADY CARMELLA," WHITMORE CALLED, his voice smooth yet carrying effortlessly over the chatter of the ballroom. "Do join us. I could not help but notice you standing alone. We wouldn't want you to feel excluded from the conversation."

Carmella hesitated, her heart quickening in her chest. She had been trying to stay unnoticed, to remain at a distance while she gathered her thoughts, but Whitmore's invitation was impossible to refuse without drawing even more attention. She forced a polite smile and moved towards him, the hem of her gown brushing against the polished floor as she stepped closer to the small group of men surrounding her father.

"Of course, Lord Whitmore," she replied, her voice steady despite the knot tightening in her stomach. "I would be glad to join you."

Whitmore's smile widened as she approached. "We were just discussing matters of some importance," he said, his gaze shifting briefly to her father, who looked distinctly uncomfortable. "Your father has been most insightful, as always."

Lord Aston gave a tight nod, his hand gripping his glass with a white-knuckled intensity. Carmella could see the strain in his face, the tension in his shoulders. "Yes, well," he muttered, avoiding her gaze, "one does what one must."

Whitmore's eyes flicked to Carmella again, his smile never wavering. "And what about you, Lady Carmella?" he asked, his tone deceptively light. "Do you find these matters of state as fascinating as your father does?"

Carmella managed a small laugh, though it felt hollow in her throat. "I am afraid my interests lie elsewhere, Lord Whitmore," she said carefully. "I am more inclined towards literature and the arts, as you may recall."

Whitmore's smile tightened just a fraction. "Ah, yes, the arts. A noble pursuit for a lady of your station. But surely you must appreciate the importance of politics, especially in these uncertain times."

She knew he was baiting her, trying to draw her into a discussion she was ill-prepared for. She glanced at her father, hoping for some guidance, but he remained silent, his eyes fixed on the floor. She felt a surge of frustration—why wouldn't he speak up? Why was he letting Whitmore play this game?

Before she could respond, Whitmore continued, his voice lowering to a more conspiratorial tone. "You see, Lady Carmella, your father and I have been discussing the future of our great nation. There are those who believe in a strong naval presence, in bolstering our forces. But others—wiser heads, some might say—believe that a different approach is needed. That perhaps we should focus on... more strategic alliances, rather than brute force. Lord Chesterfield, for one, agrees with me. I know your father has spoken with him."

Carmella's brow furrowed slightly. She knew enough about politics to understand that Whitmore was advocating for something that went against the current sentiment in many circles. She could see her father tense further, his grip on his glass tightening even more.

"I am sure my father is more qualified to speak on such matters than I am," she replied cautiously. "He has always been a man of principle."

"Indeed," Whitmore said, his smile never reaching his eyes. "And yet, principles can be... flexible, can they not? Especially when one considers the stakes."

Carmella felt a chill run down her spine. She knew exactly what Whitmore was implying, and the insinuation made her blood boil. How dare he speak of her father's principles in such a way? She glanced at her father again, willing him to say something, but he remained silent, his face drawn and pale.

Sensing the tension, Whitmore shifted the conversation again. "Perhaps we should continue this discussion somewhere a bit more private," he suggested smoothly. "The terrace, perhaps? It is a lovely evening, and the fresh air might do us all some good."

He gestured towards the open doors leading out onto the terrace. Lord Aston hesitated, his eyes darting to Carmella, then back to Whitmore. "Yes, of course," he said finally, his voice strained. "A bit of fresh air... that sounds like a good idea."

Carmella's heart sank. She knew her father was trying to play along, to buy some time, but she could see the fear in his eyes. "If you'll excuse me, Lord Whitmore," she interjected, "I believe my place is here with the other guests."

Whitmore's smile was tight. "Nonsense, my dear. Your insight would be invaluable. Besides, I wouldn't want you to feel left out." He gestured for her to join them, and she had no choice but to follow, her heart pounding as they stepped out onto the terrace.

The terrace was cooler, the night air crisp against her skin. The murmur of conversation from the ballroom faded behind them, replaced by the rustle of leaves and the distant sound of a carriage passing by on the street. Whitmore led them to a secluded corner, his demeanour calm but his eyes cold and calculating.

"Lord Aston," Whitmore began, his tone still deceptively polite, "I believe we were discussing the upcoming vote on naval funding. Your influence could be... instrumental in determining the outcome."

Her father stiffened, a muscle in his jaw twitching. "I've told you, Whitmore," he said, his voice low, "I will not support a bill that weakens our navy. It is essential to our nation's defence."

Whitmore's smile faded, his expression hardening. "You know as well as I do that there are other considerations. Financial considerations, for example. And alliances that could be jeopardised by a show of force."

Carmella's stomach churned. She could see the strain on her father's face, the way his shoulders hunched as if under a great weight. She wanted to reach out, to take his hand and offer some comfort, but she knew it would only make things worse.

"I will not betray my principles," her father said, his voice trembling but resolute.

Whitmore's eyes narrowed, and he took a step closer to Lord Aston, his tone now icy. "Principles are all well and good, Lord Aston, but they do not pay debts. And they certainly do not protect those you love from harm."

Carmella's heart froze in her chest. She knew exactly what Whitmore was implying, and the thought of him threatening her father—threatening her—filled her with a cold dread. She opened her mouth to speak, to demand he stop, but her father cut her off.

"You leave my daughter out of this," he said, his voice shaking with barely controlled anger. "Whatever you have against me, do not involve her."

Whitmore's smile returned, but it was a cruel, mocking thing. "Oh, but she is already involved, my dear Lord Aston. You see, your actions—or inactions—have consequences. And sometimes, those consequences extend beyond the person directly involved."

Carmella felt her pulse quicken, her mind racing with fear and uncertainty. She needed to do something, to find a way to protect her father, but she was trapped, caught in Whitmore's web.

Just then, the terrace doors opened, and Mrs Hunt stepped outside, her expression one of polite concern. "Lady Carmella," she called softly, her eyes flickering to the group, "I believe you were looking for me?"

Carmella seized the opportunity, turning to Whitmore with a strained smile. "If you'll excuse me, Lord Whitmore," she said, her voice steady despite the pounding of her heart. "I believe I should return to the party."

But Whitmore's smile sharpened, his eyes narrowing with an almost predatory glint. "I think not, Lady Carmella," he said smoothly, taking a step closer to her. "We were just getting to the heart of the matter. Your presence is quite essential, after all. Wouldn't you agree, Lord Aston?"

Her father shifted uncomfortably beside her, his face pale. "Perhaps it is best, Carmella, if you stay," he murmured, not meeting her eyes. "There is much to discuss."

Carmella felt a surge of panic. She glanced back at Mrs Hunt, who looked equally alarmed. "I—really, I should—"

"Nonsense," Whitmore interrupted, his tone firm but with a veneer of politeness. "I insist, my dear. After all, you are as much a part of this as your father."

Mrs Hunt stepped forward, her expression firm. "If Lady Carmella wishes to return to the party, I see no reason why she should not," she said, her voice calm but edged with authority. "This is hardly the place for such discussions."

Whitmore's eyes flicked to Mrs Hunt, his smile never faltering but his gaze turning colder. "I appreciate your concern, Mrs Hunt, but you are rather new to London affairs. The lady's presence is required. Surely you understand."

Carmella's heart raced, her mind scrambling for a way out. She couldn't leave her father alone with Whitmore, not when he was under such pressure. But she also knew that staying could mean placing herself in further danger.

Before she could decide, the terrace doors opened again, and Robert stepped out, closely followed by Captain Hunt. Robert was still in his footman's disguise, but his posture and expression were anything but subservient. "Baron Whitmore," Hunt said, his voice calm but firm, cutting through the tension like a blade. "I believe the conversation has run its course. It's time we returned to the party."

Whitmore's gaze snapped to Hunt, then shifted to Robert, his eyes narrowing. "What is this?" he sneered, his tone dripping with disdain. "A mutiny among the servants? Captain Hunt, I would advise you to keep your man in line."

Robert stood his ground, his eyes steady on Whitmore. "My apologies, sir," he said with a measured calmness, "but I believe it would be best if Lady Carmella returned inside."

Whitmore's expression darkened, his smile thinning into a hard line. "You have overstepped, footman," he hissed. "I'll see you dismissed for your insolence."

Hunt stepped forward, his presence commanding. "Whitmore, enough," he said quietly but with unmistakable authority. "Let the lady go inside. There's no need to cause a scene."

Whitmore's eyes flickered with a mix of anger and calculation. He knew he was outnumbered, but his pride wouldn't let him back down easily. "Very well," he said slowly, his voice tight with barely concealed rage. "But remember this, Hunt—and you too, footman—this is far from over. There will be consequences."

Carmella moved quickly to Robert's side. Her heart pounded in her chest, but she forced herself to remain calm. "Thank you, Captain Hunt," she said softly, her gaze flicking between him and Robert. "I appreciate your intervention."

Hunt gave her a reassuring nod. "Stay with Mrs Hunt," he advised. "We'll take care of this."

Whitmore's gaze lingered on Robert, a cold, dangerous glint in his eyes. "You've made a grave mistake tonight," he said quietly, his voice low and menacing. "Mark my words, you'll regret this."

Robert held his gaze, unflinching. "We'll see about that," he replied evenly.

As Hunt guided Whitmore away, Robert gently took Carmella's arm, leading her back inside. She could feel the tension in his grip, the barely contained fury simmering beneath his calm exterior.

"Stay close," he murmured as they slipped back into the ballroom. "Things are about to get even more dangerous."

R OBERT LED CARMELLA THROUGH the grand double doors back into the ballroom, his grip firm but gentle on her arm. He kept his expression composed, but
inside, his mind was racing. Whitmore's threats were not to be taken lightly, and he knew
the man wouldn't let this slight go unchallenged.

"Stay close to Mrs Hunt," he whispered to Carmella as they entered the crowded room.
"I'll be nearby, but we need to keep up appearances."

Carmella nodded, her eyes wide with a mixture of fear and determination. She glanced
around the room, searching for Mrs Hunt, who was now speaking with a small group
of ladies near the far wall and gesturing for Carmella to join them. Robert gave her arm
a reassuring squeeze before stepping back, blending into the throng of guests, his eyes
scanning for any sign of trouble.

He spotted Hunt and Whitmore across the room, deep in what appeared to be a heated
conversation. Hunt's posture was tense, his hands clasped behind his back as he spoke in
low, urgent tones. Whitmore's face was set in a scowl, his eyes darting around the room
as if calculating his next move.

As he approached, he could hear the tail end of Hunt's conversation with Lord Bexley.
"...all quite concerning, but we need more than rumours to act," Bexley was saying, his
tone cautious.

Hunt nodded, his expression serious. "I understand, my lord, but you must
see—Whitmore's influence over Aston is clear to any who knows him. He's not acting
of his own volition."

Robert stepped closer, catching Hunt's eye. Hunt gave a slight nod, acknowledging
him but not breaking his conversation with Bexley. Robert waited, keeping a discreet
distance, listening carefully to the murmurs around him.

Suddenly, Whitmore appeared, his face composed but his eyes burning with cold fury.
He approached Lord Bexley and Hunt with deliberate strides, a polite smile plastered on
his face. "Gentlemen," he said smoothly, "I hope I'm not interrupting?"

Lord Bexley turned to Whitmore, his expression guarded. "Not at all, Whitmore. We
were just discussing the evening's events. Quite a stir, wouldn't you say?"

Whitmore's smile tightened. "Indeed, quite a stir. I must say, I was surprised by the
commotion on the terrace. It's not often one sees a footman speaking out of turn so
boldly." His eyes flicked to Robert, a thinly veiled threat in his gaze.

Robert held Whitmore's stare, unflinching. "I was merely ensuring Lady Carmella's
safety," he said evenly. "I believe that is expected of all servants, wouldn't you agree?"

Whitmore's smile didn't reach his eyes. "Ah, but not all servants are quite so... forward," he replied. "And certainly not all have such an interest in the affairs of their betters."

Hunt interjected, his voice steady. "Whitmore, let's not make a scene here. We're all aware of the stakes, but this isn't the place for such talk."

Whitmore's gaze shifted to Hunt, his smile fading. "Captain Hunt, I've always respected your service to the Crown, but this... interference is quite out of character. I wonder what motivates it?"

Hunt met his gaze evenly. "I'm motivated by what's right, Whitmore. And by what's just. I think we both know that Lord Aston has been coerced into actions against his will. This ends tonight."

A flicker of annoyance crossed Whitmore's face. "And how do you propose to do that, Captain? With all due respect, I doubt a former military man has much sway in the matters of the House of Lords."

Lord Bexley cleared his throat. "Gentlemen, perhaps it would be best to continue this discussion in a more private setting."

Before anyone could respond, a commotion erupted from the other side of the room. Roland Hawthorne, his face flushed and eyes wild, had pushed his way through the crowd, his gaze fixed on Carmella.

"Ah, the lady of the hour!" he snarled, pointing at Carmella, his voice slurred slightly with drink. "Trying to humiliate me in front of everyone!"

Carmella took a step back, her face pale, and Mrs Hunt moved protectively in front of her. "Mr Hawthorne, you are intoxicated," Mrs Hunt said sharply. "I suggest you compose yourself."

Roland sneered. "Compose myself? This woman is to be my wife, and she thinks she can—"

"She has not agreed to anything," Robert cut in, stepping forward, his voice cold and steady. "And if you continue to make a spectacle of yourself, you'll only prove to everyone here how unfit you are to be her husband."

Roland's eyes blazed with anger. "Who are you to speak to me like that, you bloody servant?"

Robert didn't flinch. "A servant of the crown. That is who I am."

Roland lunged forward, clearly intending to strike Robert, but Robert sidestepped smoothly, catching Roland's arm and twisting it behind his back in a swift, controlled motion. The room gasped in shock, and Roland cried out in pain, dropping to his knees.

"Enough!" Whitmore barked, his voice sharp. "Release him at once, or you'll find yourself in chains!"

Robert looked up at Whitmore, his grip firm but controlled. "If you want him released, then make sure he knows his place," he said calmly. "I won't tolerate threats against Lady Carmella."

Lord Bexley, looking increasingly uncomfortable, stepped forward. "This has gone far enough," he said. "Captain Hunt, control your man, and Lord Whitmore, take your guests and leave. This is a respectable house, not a venue for your petty disputes."

Whitmore's eyes were cold and calculating as he looked from Lord Bexley to Hunt and then back to Robert. "Very well," he said softly. "But know this—you've made powerful enemies tonight. This isn't over."

He turned on his heel, and with a glare at Robert, motioned for Roland to follow him. Robert released Roland, who stumbled to his feet, shooting Robert a venomous look before slinking away.

Hunt stepped up beside Robert, his hand on his shoulder. "You humiliated the man. Whitmore won't let this slide."

Robert nodded, his eyes still on the retreating figures of Whitmore and Roland. "I know," he said quietly. "But we've bought some time. We need to use it wisely."

As the crowd slowly began to disperse, their whispers and mutterings filling the room, Robert turned back to Carmella, who was watching him with wide, grateful eyes.

"Are you well?" he asked.

She nodded. "Yes... thank you. I don't know what would have happened if you hadn't intervened."

He gave her a small, reassuring smile. "I may have made matters worse," he said. "Perhaps you can forgive me later. I'll be back soon."

As he moved away, he felt Hunt's hand grip his arm. "Daniels," Hunt said in a low voice, "we need to talk strategy. Whitmore is bound to make his move soon."

Robert nodded. "Agreed. Let's find a place to talk."

Together, they slipped away from the prying eyes of the crowd, moving toward a quieter part of the house. There was much to discuss, and they could afford no mistakes.

Chapter Eighteen

Robert took a steadying breath as he approached Lord Aston with Captain Hunt at his side. The room buzzed with the aftermath of Whitmore's confrontation, and though most of the guests were gradually returning to their conversations, there was an undercurrent of tension that hadn't dissipated.

Lord Aston stood by the far wall, his expression tight with a mixture of anxiety and anger. Robert could feel the weight of the moment pressing on his shoulders, the gravity of what he was about to confess. He glanced at Hunt, who gave him a subtle nod of encouragement. It was now or never.

"Lord Aston," Robert began, his voice steady but respectful as he came to a stop in front of the earl. "May I have a word?"

Lord Aston turned, his eyes narrowing as he took in Robert's appearance. "And who might you be, young man?" he demanded, his tone cold. "I do not recall making your acquaintance."

Robert straightened his shoulders. "Robert Daniels, my lord," he said evenly. "I served under Captain Hunt in France. And, I must confess, I am the same man who—who fled from your daughter's window two years ago."

The change in Lord Aston's demeanour was immediate and severe. His face darkened, a flush of anger rising from his neck to his cheeks. "You!" he spat, his voice low and furious. "You dare show your face here, near my daughter, after what you did? How dare you!"

Robert braced himself, meeting Aston's wrathful gaze head-on. "I understand your anger, my lord," he said quietly. "I have no excuse for my actions, but I assure you, I never intended to dishonour Lady Carmella. I... I was young and foolish, and I—"

Lord Aston cut him off with a furious wave of his hand. "You think you can come here with your apologies and excuses and think that makes up for it?" he hissed. "You have no idea the damage you caused. The scandal that nearly ensued. My daughter's reputation—"

"My lord," Hunt interjected calmly, stepping forward, his voice carrying a note of authority that seemed to cut through Aston's rage. "I understand your anger, but I can personally vouch for Mr Daniels. He served under me with honour and distinction. I only became aware of this... coincident... recently myself. Daniels is a good man, and he has only your daughter's safety in mind."

Lord Aston's eyes flicked to Hunt, his jaw clenched tightly. "A good man?" he echoed, his voice bitter. "A good man doesn't sneak into a young lady's room under the cover of darkness. A good man doesn't run like a thief in the night."

Robert felt the sting of Aston's words, but he kept his expression steady. "I was a fool," he admitted. "But I've spent every day since trying to make up for that mistake. I would never do anything to harm Lady Carmella. I only want to keep her safe. That's why I'm here."

Aston's face softened, but only slightly. He looked between Hunt and Robert, his eyes still filled with suspicion. "And why should I believe you now?" he demanded. "Why should I trust anything you say?"

Hunt placed a hand on Aston's shoulder, his expression earnest. "Because I trust him, my lord," he said. "I've seen him in the heat of battle. I've seen the sacrifices he's made for his country, for his comrades. He's a man of honour. And right now, with the information he tracked back from the Continent, he's your best chance at keeping you *and* your daughter safe."

Lord Aston's gaze lingered on Hunt's face for a long moment, then shifted back to Robert. He seemed to wrestle with himself, the anger in his eyes gradually giving way to a reluctant acceptance. "Very well," he said stiffly. "But mark my words, Daniels—I will be watching you. If you so much as breathe the wrong way around my daughter—"

Robert nodded solemnly. "I understand, my lord. And you have my word. My only concern is for Lady Carmella's safety."

Lord Aston exhaled slowly, his shoulders sagging with the weight of the evening's events. He looked around the room, his eyes settling on Carmella, who was speaking quietly with Mrs Hunt near the fireplace. "I don't like this," he muttered. "Not one bit. But if you and Hunt are offering to escort us home..."

Hunt nodded. "I think it would be wise, my lord," he said gently. "With Whitmore's men about, I wouldn't leave the duty to your footmen. Daniels and I will see you and Lady Carmella home safely."

Lord Aston's face was pale, his eyes flicking between Hunt and Robert once more before he gave a reluctant nod. "Very well," he said. "We shall leave at once."

As they moved toward the door, Robert could feel the tension still radiating off Lord Aston. The earl kept a tight grip on his daughter's arm as if afraid she might be snatched away at any moment. Robert walked a few paces behind, his eyes scanning the room for any sign of Whitmore's men. He caught Carmella's eye briefly, and she gave him a small, grateful smile.

Once outside, they made their way to the carriage waiting at the front. Robert opened the door for them, watching as Carmella and Lord Aston climbed inside. He exchanged a quick glance with Hunt, who nodded and climbed in after them.

Robert followed, pulling the door closed behind him. The carriage started off down the darkened street, the sound of the horses' hooves echoing in the quiet night. Robert could feel the tension in the air, the silence inside the carriage heavy with unspoken fears.

Lord Aston sat rigid, his eyes staring straight ahead. Carmella was beside him, her hands clasped tightly in her lap, her gaze darting nervously out the window. Hunt sat across from them, his posture relaxed but his eyes alert.

They had only been driving for a few minutes when Robert's senses prickled with the feeling of being watched. He leaned slightly toward Hunt, speaking in a low voice. "We're not alone," he murmured.

Hunt gave a slight nod. "I noticed," he replied quietly. "There's a carriage following us. Two riders alongside."

Lord Aston's head whipped around at their words, his face going pale. "What—what does this mean?" he stammered.

"It means we need to be ready," Robert said, his voice steady. "Stay calm, my lord. We're prepared for this."

The carriage suddenly lurched to a halt, and Robert's hand went instinctively to the pistol hidden beneath his coat. He met Hunt's eyes, and the captain nodded.

"Stay inside," Hunt ordered quietly, his hand already moving to the sword at his side. "Don't make a sound."

Robert pushed open the door and stepped out, Hunt right behind him. The street was dark, the only light coming from a few flickering lamps. Two men on horseback were closing in from either side, their eyes fixed on the carriage.

Robert's pulse quickened, his mind racing through possible scenarios. He could see another carriage pulling up behind theirs, blocking their retreat. The men dismounted, moving toward them with purpose, their faces shadowed but their intent clear.

One of the men drew a pistol, aiming it directly at Robert. "Stand aside, footman," he barked. "We're here for Lord Aston and his daughter. No need for you to get hurt."

Robert's eyes narrowed, his grip tightening on his own pistol. "I don't think so," he said coldly. "You'll have to get through us first."

Hunt drew his sword with a swift, practised motion, stepping forward to place himself between the attackers and the carriage. "This is your last warning," he called out. "Turn back now, or face the consequences."

The man with the pistol sneered. "Have it your way."

Robert moved instinctively, dodging to the side even before the shot rang out, the bullet whizzing past his shoulder. He raised his own pistol, firing back with precise aim. The man cried out, clutching his arm as he stumbled backwards.

Hunt charged forward, his sword flashing in the dim light as he engaged the second man. The clash of steel filled the air, the two men locked in a deadly dance. Robert turned to face the remaining attacker, his pistol still raised.

The man hesitated, his eyes flicking between Robert and the carriage. "We don't want to kill you," he said, his voice strained. "Just hand over Aston, and no one else needs to die."

Robert took a step forward, his expression hard. "That's not going to happen," he replied. "You picked the wrong carriage tonight."

Before the man could respond, Hunt's sword sliced through the air, disarming his opponent with a swift, practised stroke. The man cried out, falling to the ground clutching his wounded arm.

Robert kept his pistol trained on the remaining man, who slowly began to back away, realising the odds were no longer in his favour. "Tell Whitmore," Robert said, his voice cold and clear, "that if he wants a fight, he'll get one. But we're not going down easily."

The man gave a curt nod, his eyes wide with fear, and quickly mounted his horse, spurring it into a gallop down the dark street. Robert watched him go, his pistol still raised, until he disappeared from sight.

Hunt turned to Robert, a small, approving smile on his face. "Well done, Daniels," he said. "But we'd better get moving. This won't be the last of them."

Robert nodded, quickly reloading his pistol as he moved back to the carriage. He rapped on the door, and Carmella's face appeared in the small window, her eyes wide with worry.

"It's all right," he said, his voice gentle. "We're safe for now. But we need to keep moving."

She nodded, and Robert turned back to Hunt, his expression grim. "We need to get them somewhere safe," he said. "And fast."

Hunt nodded. "Agreed. Let's get moving. We'll figure out our next move once we're out of danger."

Robert climbed back into the carriage, taking his place beside Carmella as Hunt signalled the driver to move. The carriage lurched forward, and they set off into the night, the danger far from over, but for now, at least, they were safe.

C ARMELLA CLUTCHED ROBERT'S ARM as the carriage rattled to a stop outside their townhouse. Her heart still pounded in her chest from the attack, the chaotic sounds of the struggle echoing in her mind. She glanced at her father, who sat across from her, his face drawn and pale, a sheen of sweat on his brow. Captain Hunt was already out of the carriage, scanning the street for any sign of danger.

"Stay inside," Robert murmured to her as he followed Hunt out, his eyes sharp and alert. "We need to make sure it's safe first."

Carmella nodded, but her hand tightened on her reticule, her knuckles white. She watched as Robert and Hunt moved swiftly, checking the front door, the windows, every possible entry point. She could see the tension in Robert's posture, the way his hand hovered near his coat pocket, ready for anything.

Her father shifted beside her, his eyes flicking nervously between the men outside and the interior of the carriage. He seemed smaller than usual, diminished somehow, his shoulders slumped. "I should never have let it get this far," he muttered, almost to himself.

Carmella turned to him, her voice soft but firm. "Father, how did you become indebted to Whitmore? Why did he threaten you like that?"

Lord Aston's gaze snapped to hers, and for a moment, she saw a flicker of something—fear, regret, shame. "It's complicated," he said finally, his voice hoarse. "But you must understand, Carmella, everything I've done... I did it for you. For our family."

Before she could press him further, Robert opened the carriage door and offered his hand. "It's clear, for now," he said. "But we need to get inside."

Carmella took his hand, feeling the roughness of his skin against hers, and stepped out onto the pavement. Her father followed, his movements slow and hesitant. Once inside, Robert and Hunt quickly bolted the door behind them, locking the world—and the danger—outside.

Captain Hunt gave a quick nod to Robert, who immediately began to check the windows again, ensuring they were secure. "We don't have much time," Hunt said quietly, his gaze shifting to Lord Aston. "We need to know everything, my lord."

Carmella watched her father, her heart aching with a mix of worry and frustration. "Please, Father," she urged. "You have to tell us what's been happening. We can't help if we don't know the truth."

Lord Aston seemed to sag further into himself, as if the weight of his secrets was finally too much to bear. He sank into a nearby chair, his hands trembling slightly. "It started with a business venture," he began, his voice barely above a whisper. "A shipping company. Lord Chesterfield told me about it first, and then Whitmore and Hawthorne went in for it. Or said they did... I was convinced it would turn a profit, that it was a safe investment. But... I was wrong."

Carmella listened, her breath catching in her throat. She had known her father was struggling, but she hadn't realised the extent. "And Whitmore?" she prompted gently. "How did he come into it?"

Lord Aston looked down at his hands, his fingers twisting nervously. "Whitmore has a way of finding out about men's troubles," he said bitterly. "He offered to help—to cover my debts, to keep my creditors at bay. In return, he asked for a few favours. At first, it seemed harmless enough... introductions, letters of recommendation. But then, his demands grew."

Captain Hunt crossed his arms, his expression grim. "He used your debts to manipulate you. To gain influence in the House of Lords."

"Yes," Lord Aston admitted, his voice cracking with emotion. "He wanted me to oppose certain measures, to speak against funding for the navy. I didn't realise at first what he was planning. But by the time I did, it was too late. He had too much on me. And then... then he threatened you, Carmella."

"Me? Why?"

"To ensure my compliance," her father replied, his voice thick with guilt. "He knew I would do anything to protect you. It was his idea to engage you to Hawthorne—friend of his, do you see? I thought that was the least of the concessions—thought Hawthorne was a decent enough chap. No title, but wealthy enough to give you the life you were accustomed to. But when you started asking questions, when you protested the engagement... he saw it as a threat. He said he would ruin us both if I didn't do as he asked."

Carmella's heart ached for her father, seeing him like this—so vulnerable, so filled with regret. She reached out, placing a comforting hand on his arm. "Father, we can still fix this," she said softly. "Robert and Captain Hunt are here to help. We're not alone."

Robert moved closer, his expression serious but determined. "We need to expose Whitmore's schemes, publicly and decisively," he said. "We need to show everyone what he's been doing—how he's been manipulating people like you."

Lord Aston nodded, though he still looked uncertain. "But how? He's covered his tracks well. And his men... they'll do anything to protect him. You saw that ten minutes ago."

"We'll find a way," Hunt interjected firmly. "But we need you to be strong, my lord. This is our chance to set things right."

Just then, a sharp knock at the door made them all jump. Robert and Hunt exchanged a quick glance, both of them moving swiftly to stand by the entrance. Robert placed a finger to his lips, signalling for silence, then slowly approached the door, his hand on his weapon.

Carmella's heart pounded in her chest, her eyes wide as she watched Robert. The knock came again, more insistent this time. She held her breath, praying it wasn't more of Whitmore's men.

Robert leaned close to the door, listening for any sounds outside. After a tense moment, he turned the latch and slowly opened the door a crack, peering out.

"Who is it?" Carmella whispered, her voice barely audible.

Robert glanced back at her, his expression grim. "A messenger," he said quietly. "With a letter... for Lord Aston."

Lord Aston rose from his chair, his face pale. "From whom?"

Robert took the letter, examining the seal. "It's from Whitmore," he said, his voice low.

Carmella exchanged a worried look with her father as Robert handed him the letter. Lord Aston hesitated for a moment, then broke the seal and unfolded the paper. His eyes scanned the words, his expression growing darker with each passing second.

"What does it say?" Hunt asked, his tone tense.

Lord Aston swallowed hard, his hand trembling as he lowered the letter. "He's demanding a meeting," he said. "Tonight. At his estate."

Carmella felt a surge of fear, her heart clenching in her chest. "Father, no... it's a trap. You cannot go."

Lord Aston looked up at her, his eyes filled with a mixture of fear and resignation. "I have no choice," he replied quietly. "If I don't... he'll ruin us. And he's threatened to harm you."

Robert stepped forward, his jaw set. "You're not going alone," he said firmly. "Hunt and I will go with you. We'll make sure you're safe."

Lord Aston hesitated, then nodded slowly. "Very well," he agreed. "But be careful. Whitmore is dangerous... and desperate."

Carmella's heart pounded in her chest as she watched the three men prepare. She knew the stakes were high, but she also knew that Robert was right—they couldn't let Whitmore continue to control their lives. They had to end this, once and for all.

As Robert and Hunt moved toward the door, Robert turned back to her, his gaze intense. "Stay here," he instructed. "Lock the doors, and don't let anyone in."

Carmella nodded, her voice barely a whisper. "Be careful," she said, her eyes filled with worry.

Robert gave her a small, reassuring smile. "I will," he promised. "We'll finish this."

Chapter Nineteen

THE DRAWING ROOM FELT emptier than ever after Robert, Captain Hunt, and her father had left. Carmella paced the length of the room, her thoughts swirling like a storm. She could still feel the tension in the air, lingering like a ghost after their hurried departure. She had tried to focus on something, anything, to keep herself grounded, but her mind kept returning to the fear in her father's eyes, the firm set of Robert's jaw, the looming threat of Whitmore.

Unable to sit still any longer, she found herself drawn back to her father's desk. It loomed in the corner, a dark, imposing presence that seemed to hold all the answers she desperately needed. Her eyes were drawn to the slightly ajar drawer, the same one where she had found the letter that had exposed Whitmore's schemes. She hesitated for a moment, her heart pounding. She knew it was wrong to snoop through her father's things, but she also knew that she couldn't let this opportunity slip by. If there was something here, something that could help them…

She reached out and pulled the drawer open further, her breath catching in her throat. The papers inside were a chaotic mess, as if her father had hastily shoved them in, trying to hide them from prying eyes. Her fingers trembled as she began to sift through them. Receipts, bills, correspondence—nothing out of the ordinary at first. But then, her hand brushed against a folded sheet of paper, tucked between the pages of an old ledger.

With a quick glance over her shoulder to ensure she was still alone, she unfolded the paper and began to read. It wasn't a simple note like before. This was a detailed letter, written in a hurried, almost frantic hand, filled with figures and instructions. The further she read, the more her stomach twisted into knots.

The letter laid everything out in stark detail—exactly what her father was expected to do, the votes he was to sway in the House of Lords, the influence he was to exert against naval spending. It even detailed the amount of debt her father had accumulated, the astronomical sums he owed, and the threats Whitmore had made should he fail to comply.

Carmella's hand tightened on the letter, crumpling the edges. This was more than just coercion; it was blackmail on a grand scale. Whitmore held her father's entire future—his reputation, his finances, his very freedom—in his hands. And her father had felt he had no choice but to obey.

Her breath came in short, shallow gasps as she read on. Whitmore was taking his orders from Chesterfield, and they were both using her father to undermine naval efforts, weakening their defences while lining his own pockets. It was treason, plain and simple. And her father had been trapped in it. She felt a surge of anger, hot and fierce, burning away the fear that had held her captive. This was more than her father's shameful secret—this was a matter of national security.

Oh, why had her father not thought to show this to Captain Hunt? This was precisely what they needed as proof! She had to act. She couldn't just wait here while Robert and Hunt confronted Whitmore. She needed someone with real authority, someone who could bear witness to this treachery and take swift action. But who? Her aunt Eleanor had left for Sussex, and most of her father's political allies were either compromised or too cowardly to stand up to Whitmore.

Then, it struck her. Lord Farnsworth—the elderly gentleman who lived in the townhouse next door. He was a venerable member of the House of Lords, a man of integrity who had always been kind to her. Though he rarely attended society events these days, he was well respected and had the ear of the Prince Regent himself. If anyone could help, it was him.

Her mind raced with the possibilities. If she could persuade Lord Farnsworth to accompany her, to see for himself the evidence of Whitmore's schemes, perhaps they could expose Whitmore's machinations publicly. Her father might not have the strength to stand against Whitmore alone, but with a powerful ally...

She took a deep breath, steeling herself. It was a bold move, but she had no choice. She could not sit idly by while her father and Robert risked everything. She needed to take action, to do something meaningful. She glanced at the clock on the mantel. It was late, but not so late that a visit would be entirely improper, especially given the urgency of the matter.

Quickly, she tucked the letter into the pocket of her gown and hurried to the door. She opened it just a crack, peering out into the hallway. "Thomas!" she called softly, hoping the butler was still nearby.

A moment later, the butler appeared, his expression one of concern. "Yes, my lady?" he asked.

"Thomas, I need you to accompany me next door to Lord Farnsworth's townhouse," she said, trying to keep her voice steady. "There is something urgent I must discuss with him."

The butler hesitated, clearly taken aback by her request. "At this hour, my lady?"

"Yes, at this hour," she replied firmly. "It cannot wait."

He hesitated for a moment longer, then nodded. "Very well, my lady. I shall fetch your cloak."

She waited, her heart thudding in her chest. Was she doing the right thing? Would Lord Farnsworth even be willing to see her at this time of night? But she couldn't let doubt stop her now. She had to believe that he would understand the gravity of the situation.

When Thomas returned with her cloak, she draped it over her shoulders and hurried out of the house. She glanced back once at her father's empty study, her resolve hardening. She would not let him face this alone.

They crossed the short distance to Lord Farnsworth's townhouse quickly. The imposing front door loomed before her, its brass knocker glinting in the moonlight. She hesitated for a moment, then lifted the knocker and let it fall with a solid, resounding thud.

For a moment, there was nothing. The house seemed eerily quiet, as if the very walls were holding their breath. Then, slowly, the door creaked open, and a stern-faced butler peered out at them.

"Lady Carmella?" he asked, clearly surprised to see her. "Is something amiss?"

"Yes, there is," Carmella said quickly. "I need to speak with Lord Farnsworth. It is of the utmost importance."

The butler frowned, clearly uncertain. "His lordship is resting, my lady. It is rather late..."

"Please," Carmella urged, her voice trembling slightly. "Tell him it's about Baron Whitmore. He will understand."

The butler's eyes widened slightly at the mention of Whitmore, and he nodded. "Very well, my lady. Please, come in."

He stepped aside, allowing Carmella and Thomas to enter the dimly lit foyer. She stood there, her hands clasped tightly together, waiting as the butler disappeared up the grand staircase. She could hear the soft murmur of voices upstairs, the faint creak of floorboards, and then, after what felt like an eternity, the sound of footsteps descending.

Lord Farnsworth appeared at the top of the stairs, his figure silhouetted against the light from the upper floor. He was an older man, with a shock of white hair and a cane that clicked softly against the polished wood as he made his way down. His expression was stern, but there was a glimmer of curiosity in his eyes.

"Lady Carmella," he said, his voice warm despite his stern appearance. "What brings you here at such an hour? I trust you have a good reason."

Carmella stepped forward, holding out the crumpled letter. "I do, my lord," she said, her voice steady. "I need your help. It's about my father... and Baron Whitmore."

Lord Farnsworth's brows drew together as he took the letter from her hand. He unfolded it carefully, his eyes scanning the contents. As he read, his expression grew more serious, his jaw tightening.

"This is... significant," he said quietly, his eyes lifting to meet hers. "And you believe your father is involved?"

Carmella nodded, her heart pounding. "He is... but not by choice. Whitmore has been blackmailing him, forcing him to act against his will. I fear for his safety, my lord. And for the safety of others."

Lord Farnsworth's eyes narrowed, and he nodded slowly. "Very well," he said, his voice firm. "I will accompany you. If what you say is true, this matter requires immediate attention."

Relief flooded through her, and she felt a surge of gratitude. "Thank you, my lord," she said softly. "I knew I could count on you."

He offered her a small, reassuring smile. "We must act quickly," he said. "Time is of the essence."

With that, he turned to the butler. "Prepare the carriage, Thomas. We leave at once."

R OBERT, HUNT, AND LORD Aston stepped out of the carriage onto the gravel drive of Whitmore's Hampstead estate, the crunch of stones beneath their boots the only sound in the still night. The manor loomed before them, its grand arches and high windows casting dark shadows that seemed to swallow the dim light of the carriage lamps. Robert scanned the grounds with a practised eye, noting the presence of Whitmore's men stationed discreetly around the perimeter, their postures alert and eyes watchful.

Hunt gave a subtle nod to Robert as the heavy oak door swung open. A butler appeared, his face expressionless, though his eyes flickered with recognition and a hint of suspicion as they lingered on Robert. "Lord Aston, Captain Hunt," he greeted them with a stiff bow. "Lord Whitmore is expecting you. Please follow me."

Robert kept his face carefully neutral, his senses on high alert as they were led through the grand entrance hall and into a lavishly decorated drawing room. The rich tapestries and heavy drapes did little to soften the cold, austere atmosphere of the manor. Whitmore stood by the fireplace, his back to them, one hand resting casually on the mantel. As they entered, he turned slowly, a thin smile playing at his lips.

"Lord Aston," Whitmore said, his voice smooth and patronizing. "And I see you've brought your lapdog. Good evening again, Captain Hunt." His gaze shifted to Robert, his eyes narrowing slightly. "And I do not believe we have been introduced. You are certainly not one of Bexley's footmen, are you?"

Robert stepped forward, meeting Whitmore's gaze with a steady calm. "I am sure you will forget my name the minute I give it, so I shan't bother. We're here to discuss your dealings, Whitmore," he said, his tone firm but controlled. "And the way you've manipulated Lord Aston into betraying his country's interests."

Whitmore's smile widened, a mocking glint in his eyes. "Manipulated? Oh, you give me far too much credit," he replied, his tone dripping with feigned humility. "Lord Aston is a man of his own mind. He's simply made a few... strategic decisions."

Lord Aston's face flushed, a mix of anger and shame clouding his features. "You've twisted my arm, Whitmore," he said, his voice trembling with barely suppressed rage. "Forced me into a corner with your threats and deceit. I refuse to be your pawn any longer."

Whitmore's expression remained calm, though his eyes flickered with a hint of irritation. "Threats? Deceit? My dear Aston, I merely offered you opportunities—opportunities that you gladly took. Let's not pretend you didn't benefit."

Robert could feel the frustration building inside him. Whitmore was slippery, a master at twisting words to suit his narrative. He needed to force him into a corner, make him slip. "Enough with the games, Whitmore," Robert said sharply. "We know about your plans to manipulate naval funding for your own gain. And we have evidence that links you directly to treasonous activity."

For the first time, Whitmore's confidence seemed to waver, his smile faltering. "Evidence?" he echoed, his voice losing some of its smoothness. "What evidence?"

Before Robert could answer, the doors to the drawing room opened again. A figure stepped in—a servant, visibly nervous, his eyes darting around the room. "My lord," he stammered, "Lady Carmella is here. She insists on speaking with you."

Robert's heart skipped a beat. Carmella? *Here?* Why would she take such a risk? She must have found something significant—something that couldn't wait. He exchanged a quick glance with Hunt, who nodded slightly, understanding the unspoken urgency.

Whitmore's expression darkened, his calm façade cracking. "What is she doing here?" he demanded.

Ignoring Whitmore, Robert turned and quickly strode out of the room. He could see Carmella standing just inside the entrance hall with an older man by her side. Carmella clutched a letter tightly, her face pale. "Carmella!" he called out, hurrying toward her. "What's happened? Why are you here? And... forgive me, sir, we have not been introduced."

The man straightened his ageing spine, his gaze already floating over Robert's head. "Lord Farnsworth, sir, and you are?"

Carmella put a hand out to insert herself between them. "Lord Farnsworth, this is Sergeant Robert Daniels, the man I told you about," she said hastily. "Robert, Lord Farnsworth is my neighbour, and I asked for his help.

"Help? With what?"

She held out a folded paper. "I found this—it's a letter from Lord Chesterfield that mentions Lord Whitmore. It contains everything we need—all the proof."

Robert took the letter from her, his eyes quickly scanning the contents. It was all there: the debts, the bribes, the detailed instructions to manipulate naval funding—laid bare in Whitmore's own hand. A surge of triumph coursed through him. "You've done brilliantly," he said quietly, looking up at her with a newfound admiration. "This is exactly what we needed."

Carmella nodded, though her eyes were still filled with concern. "I knew I had to act. I couldn't just sit by any longer."

Lord Farnsworth cleared his throat. "Is it true, Lord Aston?" he asked, his voice steady but commanding. "Have you truly been involved in this?"

Lord Aston, who had just entered the hall with Hunt, turned to face his neighbour, his face a mixture of shame and resolve. "It is true," he confessed, his voice breaking slightly. "Whitmore blackmailed me, forced my hand. I... I couldn't see a way out. But I cannot let this continue. I understand I shall be censured, but—"

Farnsworth looked taken aback, his eyes narrowing with a mix of disappointment and concern. "You should have come to me, Aston. We could have found a way to manage this—honourably."

Whitmore appeared in the doorway, his face a mask of cold fury. "And what do you think you're going to do with that letter?" he sneered, stepping forward with a menacing glare. "You think a few pieces of paper will bring me down?"

Robert's attention shifted as he heard a scuffle near the doorway. Roland Hawthorne stepped into the room, his expression taut, his gaze flitting between the assembled group. "What's this, then?" he asked, a forced casualness in his tone that didn't quite mask his unease. "A little gathering without me?" He offered a strained smile, but it was clear he sensed the tension in the air, sensed the shift in power that was slipping from his grasp. His eyes settled on Carmella, his face hardening as realisation dawned. "What are you doing here?" he demanded, frustration creeping into his voice, "What have you told them?"

Robert turned slightly, positioning himself between Carmella and Roland. Carmella met Roland's gaze, her chin lifting with quiet defiance. "I've told them everything, Mr Hawthorne," she said calmly, though her voice trembled just a little. "Everything you and Lord Whitmore have been doing."

Roland's face twisted with anger, his eyes narrowing to slits. "You think you can ruin us with a few words?" he snapped, taking a step closer. "You think they'll believe you over me, over Whitmore?"

Carmella held her ground, her expression steady. "It's not about belief," she replied softly. "It's about the truth. And the truth is, your lies have caught up with you."

Roland's composure broke, his face reddening with rage. He lunged forward, but Robert moved swiftly, stepping in front of Carmella, blocking Roland's advance with a firm hand on his chest.

"That's enough," Robert said, his voice low and commanding. "You've done enough harm for one night."

Roland's face contorted with rage, and he lunged at Robert, trying to snatch the letter from his hand. Robert sidestepped quickly, and with a swift move, he grabbed Roland's arm, twisting it behind his back with a practiced motion. Robert growled, his voice low but filled with authority. "You're out of your depth, Roland. Stand down."

Roland struggled against Robert's grip, his face red with exertion and humiliation. "You'll regret this!" he shouted. "I swear it!"

Whitmore, seeing his ally restrained, took a step back, his eyes darting around the room, calculating his next move. But he was caught off guard as Hunt stepped forward, drawing his sword just enough to make his point clear. "It's over, Whitmore," Hunt said, his voice calm but deadly serious. "Enough people know what you're about."

Whitmore's face twisted with fury, but he forced a smile. "You think you've won? You've proven nothing. I still have connections."

Farnsworth stepped forward, his voice cold and authoritative. "Not after tonight, Whitmore. I've heard enough. This letter is going directly to the Prince Regent. You've overplayed your hand."

Whitmore's bravado faltered. His eyes flicked from Lord Farnsworth to Lord Aston, then back to Robert. He knew he was trapped. "Aston, you would not countenance this, surely! You would implicate yourself just to defy me?"

Aston, now standing beside Farnsworth, his shame replaced by a grim determination, spoke up. "I will, Whitmore. I'll make a full confession if it means protecting my daughter and seeing you brought to justice."

For a moment, there was silence. Then, in a final act of desperation, Whitmore lunged toward Carmella, his hand outstretched to seize the letter. But Robert was faster. He released Roland and stepped in front of Carmella, catching Whitmore's wrist in a vice-like grip.

"That's enough," Robert said, his voice steady. "It's over, Whitmore. You can't talk your way out of this."

Whitmore jerked against Robert's grip, his face twisted with frustration. "You think you can win?" he growled, his voice lower now, laced with fury. "You're a... a servant! How dare you put your hands on me?"

Captain Hunt chuckled. "That, sir, is one of the most distinguished officers ever to swear his oath to His Majesty. If even half his meritorious service were a matter of public record, his chest would be covered in so many medals it would blind you. I suggest doing as the Lieutenant says."

Whitmore blinked—first at Hunt, then at Daniels.

Robert tightened his hold on Whitmore's arm. "It's time to let this go," he said calmly. "Before you make things worse."

Whitmore glanced around the room, his gaze sweeping over the remaining occupants who were now staring at him with a mix of curiosity and disdain. His defiance faltered. With a final, furious glare, he pulled his arm free and turned sharply on his heel, marching toward the door.

Chapter Twenty

THE LATE MORNING SUN filtered softly through the lace curtains of Lord Aston's townhouse drawing room, casting delicate patterns on the polished floor. The air was thick with an uncomfortable sense of uncertainty, mingling with the scent of freshly brewed tea that had gone untouched on the table before them. Carmella sat near the window, her hands clasped tightly in her lap, her posture stiff but composed. She could hear the faint sounds of the bustling London streets outside, a stark contrast to the heavy silence that hung in the room.

Captain Hunt and Lord Farnsworth were seated nearby, each holding a cup of tea, though neither had taken a sip. Hunt, ever the soldier, sat with a quiet strength, his eyes focused on Lord Aston, who occupied a chair opposite them. Farnsworth, with his years of political manoeuvring and keen understanding of the social undercurrents of the aristocracy, wore a thoughtful expression as he observed the gathering. Lord Aston looked older than his years today, his face lined with worry and shame, his hands trembling slightly as he gripped the armrests of his chair. The ordeal of the past few days had clearly taken its toll on him.

Carmella glanced at her father, her heart aching at the sight of his frailty. Despite everything—his mistakes, his misjudgments—he was still her father. She knew that what had transpired had not been solely his fault. Whitmore had preyed upon his vulnerabilities, his desperation. She wished she could reach out to him, comfort him somehow, but she wasn't sure he would welcome her sympathy. Not after everything that had happened.

Captain Hunt was the first to break the silence. "Whitmore has been taken into custody," he said, his words measured, as though delivering a report from the battlefield.

"Thanks to the evidence you provided, Lady Carmella, along with the testimonies we gave, his crimes are undeniable. The charges include bribery, blackmail, conspiracy—each one carrying a severe penalty."

Farnsworth nodded, his expression grave. "Whitmore's influence within the House of Lords was substantial, but even his connections won't be enough to save him this time. The Prince Regent was livid when I spoke with him last night. He has ordered a thorough investigation into all of Whitmore's dealings. The man will likely face imprisonment, the stripping of his title, and the forfeiture of his lands. He will not recover from this. Chesterfield... well, he may be more difficult."

"Why is that?" Carmella asked.

Hunt uncrossed his boots with a smug look. "He took his own life last night. A shame, that. But he cannot threaten your father any longer."

Carmella felt a surge of relief at Farnsworth's words, but also a twinge of unease. The consequences for Whitmore were severe, but necessary. Still, the implications for her father's reputation were troubling. "And what of my father?" she asked softly, her voice barely above a whisper. "What happens to him now?"

Lord Farnsworth turned his attention to her, his gaze softening slightly. "Your father's situation is more complex," he said carefully. "While his cooperation with Whitmore's schemes was clearly under duress, the fact remains that he was complicit in activities that could be construed as fraudulent. However, given his willingness to testify against Whitmore and his transparency in these proceedings, I have decided to petition the Prince Regent on his behalf. I believe there is a case to be made for leniency, considering the circumstances."

Lord Aston's eyes flickered with a mixture of hope and despair. "Leniency?" he echoed, his voice rough. "And what would that entail, Lord Farnsworth? I am not blind to my own failings. I know I have disgraced my name, my family... I would not be surprised if they stripped me of my title altogether."

Farnsworth shook his head gently. "I do not believe it will come to that," he said. "The Prince is more inclined toward mercy in this instance, especially given the political advantage of exposing Whitmore. However, there will be repercussions. You may be asked to step down from certain committees, and you will undoubtedly face scrutiny from your peers. Your debts, I fear, are another matter entirely."

Aston's face tightened, and he looked down, unable to meet their eyes. "The debts," he murmured, his voice heavy with resignation. "I had hoped to find a way to pay them off without resorting to Whitmore's schemes. But when the investments failed..." He trailed off, the weight of his decisions pressing down upon him. "I've nothing left. The townhouse, perhaps, and what remains of the estate in Sussex. But it is not enough."

Carmella felt a pang of sadness for her father. She knew how much his pride meant to him, how difficult it was for him to admit defeat. She reached for his hand, covering it with her own. "We'll find a way, Father," she said gently. "There are still options. We can sell the townhouse. Move to Sussex. Live more modestly."

Aston looked up, his eyes meeting hers for the first time. There was a flicker of gratitude in his gaze, mixed with the deep-seated sorrow of a man who had lost much. "You are too kind, Carmella," he said softly. "But I fear I have little to offer you now. Your dowry... I had hoped to secure a future for you, a good match. But now..."

She squeezed his hand, her resolve firm. "My dowry is still intact," she said, a touch of defiance in her tone. "I made sure of that. And as for a 'good match'—why, I think there is not a single 'gentleman of repute' in London who would deign to unite himself to our family just now. But that does not trouble me overmuch. I have never cared for the wealth or status of a suitor, only his character."

There was a brief silence, broken only by the soft clink of teacups as Hunt set his down on the table. "Well spoken, Lady Carmella," he said with a faint smile. "And, if I may speak frankly, Lord Aston—your daughter is more than capable of making her own choices. She has shown remarkable strength and wisdom throughout this ordeal."

Aston nodded slowly, his expression softening. "You are right, Captain Hunt," he said quietly. "I have underestimated her, as I have underestimated much of the world around me. It seems my arrogance has cost me dearly."

Hunt leaned forward, his tone gentle but firm. "Your mistakes do not define you, Lord Aston. What matters now is how you move forward. You have an opportunity to set things right, to rebuild what was lost—not just for yourself, but for Lady Carmella as well."

Farnsworth cleared his throat. "As for the estate in Sussex," he said, "it could be salvaged if managed properly. The land itself is still valuable. If you are willing to sell the townhouse and reduce your expenses, you could maintain a comfortable life there, away from the scrutiny of London. And with Lady Carmella's dowry preserved, there is a future for her, should she choose to marry."

Aston looked at Farnsworth, his expression one of reluctant acceptance. "I will consider it," he said slowly. "But I cannot ignore the fact that I have failed as a father. I wanted so much for her—everything I could not achieve myself. And now..."

Carmella's heart softened at his words. She rose from her seat and moved to her father's side, kneeling beside his chair. "You have not failed me, Father," she said quietly. "What I want—what I have always wanted—is to live a life of integrity and love. I do not need wealth or status to be happy. I only need to know that those I love are safe and cared for."

Aston looked down at her, his eyes glistening with unshed tears. "You are a better person than I, Carmella," he whispered. "I only hope I can find a way to make amends."

Robert, who had been standing quietly near the window, finally spoke, his voice steady. "There is still time to make things right, my lord," he said. "And you won't be alone. You have Lady Carmella, and you have us." He glanced at Hunt, who nodded in agreement. "We'll help you through this, in any way we can."

Aston studied Robert for a long moment, his gaze searching. "You are the man who fled from my daughter's room," he said, his voice low but not without a hint of grudging respect. "And yet, here you stand, willing to help the very family you once sought to disrupt."

Robert met Aston's gaze evenly, his expression sincere. "I am not proud of how I left things, my lord," he admitted. "But I have always cared for Lady Carmella. I left to prove myself worthy, though I see now that my departure only caused more harm than good. I want to make things right, not only for her but for you as well."

Aston's eyes softened, and he nodded slowly. "Perhaps... perhaps I misjudged you, Mr Daniels," he said. "If Captain Hunt vouches for your character, then I suppose I have no reason to doubt you. But tell me—what are your intentions now? Toward my daughter?"

Robert's gaze flickered to Carmella, who was still kneeling beside her father, her face filled with quiet hope. "My intentions," he said slowly, "are to offer her whatever future she desires. If she will have me, I would be honoured to stand by her side, to build a life together. But that is a decision only she can make."

Aston glanced at Carmella, his expression conflicted. "You love him," he said softly, more a statement than a question.

Carmella nodded, her heart full. "I do, Father. I always have."

Aston closed his eyes for a moment, then opened them, his gaze clear. "Then it is settled," he said with a sigh. "If you believe Mr Daniels is the right man for you, then I will not stand in your way."

Tears welled in Carmella's eyes as she rose to her feet, embracing her father. "Thank you," she whispered, her voice filled with emotion. "Thank you for understanding."

Farnsworth cleared his throat, breaking the tender moment. "I believe we have much to discuss regarding the practicalities," he said gently. "There will be a need to address your debts, Lord Aston, and to plan for your future in Sussex. But I am confident we can find a way to make this work."

Aston nodded, his expression resolute. "Yes," he agreed. "It is time to face my responsibilities and to rebuild what I can. And with all of your help, I am certain we will manage."

Hunt stood, extending his hand to Aston. "We'll see it through together," he said firmly. "You have my word."

Aston took Hunt's hand, a spark of hope returning to his eyes. "Thank you, Captain," he said sincerely. "Thank you all."

Carmella felt a wave of relief wash over her. For the first time in weeks, she felt a sense of peace, of closure. The future was uncertain, yes, but it was also full of possibility. She looked at Robert, who was watching her with a mixture of love and admiration, and she knew that whatever lay ahead, they would face it together.

The room gradually filled with a sense of calm determination as they began to make plans, discuss the logistics of the move to Sussex, and consider how best to settle Aston's debts. The townhouse would be sold, and with Farnsworth's assistance, the estate could be managed more effectively. They spoke of modest living, of rebuilding with dignity and honour, and for the first time in what felt like an eternity, Carmella dared to dream of a future filled with love, honesty, and the quiet joys of a simpler life.

As the conversation continued, Carmella felt Robert's hand gently take hers under the table, a silent promise of the life they were about to build together. She squeezed his hand in return, a smile touching her lips. No matter the challenges that lay ahead, she knew they would face them side by side.

And for now, that was enough.

Epilogue

T HE SUN HAD JUST begun its ascent over the rolling hills of Sussex, casting a soft golden light across the landscape. Robert stood at the edge of the garden, his gaze drifting over the fields that stretched out before him. The estate was modest by most standards, but to him, it was a palace. He took a deep breath, inhaling the fresh country air, and felt a profound sense of peace settle over him.

It had been a year since that tumultuous evening at Baron Whitmore's estate, a year since everything had changed. He still marvelled at how swiftly life could turn, how fortunes could shift like the tides. His hand instinctively went to the small scar just above his right eyebrow, a remnant from that night—a reminder of how close he'd come to losing everything he now cherished.

The manor house behind him was a warm, welcoming sight. It was not grand, but it was theirs. After selling the London townhouse and managing the debts, they had enough to live simply here, surrounded by the natural beauty of the countryside. Robert had grown to love this place, its quiet strength, its resilience. It was a far cry from the bustling streets of London or the battlefields of the Continent, but it was precisely what he needed. What they both needed.

His mother's cottage was just down the lane, not far from the main house. He could see a faint wisp of smoke rising from the chimney, a sign that she was already up and about, likely preparing breakfast. He smiled to himself, remembering the first time Carmella had met his mother as his wife. The two women had embraced as if they were long-lost friends, and from that day on, they had become inseparable. His mother adored Carmella, often recounting to him the many kindnesses she had shown over the years with those baskets she sent. It warmed his heart to know that his mother was finally content, her face no longer shadowed with worry or loneliness.

He turned at the sound of light footsteps on the gravel path. Carmella approached, her gown flowing softly around her as she moved. Her hair, loosely pinned back, caught the morning light, giving her an almost ethereal glow. She carried a small basket filled with fresh eggs, a testament to the simple, wholesome life they had built together.

"Good morning," she said, her voice bright and full of warmth. She came to stand beside him, her eyes following his gaze out over the fields. "You're up early."

"I couldn't sleep," he replied, his hand reaching for hers. "I wanted to see the morning. To remind myself how far we've come."

She smiled, leaning her head against his shoulder. "We have come far, haven't we?"

He nodded, his thumb brushing over her knuckles. "More than I ever imagined possible. There were days I thought I'd never find my way back to you, that I'd never be worthy of this." He gestured to the land around them, the home they had created and the garden they both loved. "Of you."

Carmella turned to face him, her expression tender. "You've always been worthy, Robert. Even when you didn't believe it yourself." She placed a hand on his cheek, her touch gentle. "And I never stopped believing in you."

He pulled her into his arms, holding her close. The scent of lavender clung to her hair, mingling with the fresh morning air. "I love you," he murmured, his lips brushing against her temple.

She smiled against his chest. "I love you too."

They stood there for a moment, wrapped in each other's warmth, before Carmella pulled back slightly, her eyes twinkling with mischief. "Now, come along for a little walk with me."

He let her tug on his hand, but did not move at first. "A walk? Where are we going?"

"Just down the lane and back before Cook has breakfast ready. And hurry up, soldier. I do not intend to eat cold porridge."

"Nothing worse," he agreed. "Not that I would know, of course."

She laughed. "I imagine you had all manner of cold vittles when you were in uniform! Tell me, what was the worst?"

He puckered his mouth in thought as her hand tightened through the crook of his arm. "North's carrot stew. Even the horses hated it—particularly Captain Hunt's horse Bess."

Carmella made a face. "He did *not* name his horse after his wife."

"No." Robert laughed. "North and I did... without even realising it. North hated that horse."

"Why? What was wrong with her?"

Robert paused to smile down into her beloved face. "I suppose because she chose the one man who would own her heart, and it wasn't Owen North."

"Well." Carmella stood on her toes to kiss him. "I can understand that sentiment. Oh! I nearly forgot." Carmella reached inside the pocket of her walking dress, pulling out a letter. "This was on the tray for you just before we left, Robert. It says it is from Commander North."

Robert's brows lifted in surprise. "North?" he said, taking the letter from her. "I haven't heard from him in months."

He broke the seal and unfolded the letter, his eyes scanning the familiar handwriting. As he read, his expression grew thoughtful, his fingers tightening slightly around the paper.

"What is it?" Carmella asked, her tone curious.

Robert glanced up, his eyes meeting hers. "He's asking if I'd consider taking on another assignment. Something discreet, for king and country."

Carmella rose from her seat and moved to his side, plucking the letter from his hands. "Another assignment?" she teased, holding it just out of his reach. "And what exactly does Commander North think he can tempt you with now that you've found a life of peace and comfort here?" Her tone was playful, but there was a hint of genuine curiosity beneath it.

Robert chuckled, reaching for the letter, but she pulled it away with a grin. "I suppose he thinks I might miss the old days—the thrill of the chase, the excitement of a good hunt." He paused, his smile fading slightly. "But he'd be wrong."

Carmella looked at him, her eyes searching his. "And do you?" she asked softly. "Miss it?"

Robert shook his head, his expression earnest. "No, not anymore. I've had my fill of danger and uncertainty. I'd much rather spend my days here, with you." He leaned forward, capturing her lips in a tender kiss. "Besides," he murmured against her mouth, "I keep waiting for you to write my story in one of your books."

She laughed, a light, joyous sound that filled the room. "Oh, is that what you're hoping for? To be the hero in one of my tales?"

He grinned, his hands slipping around her waist. "Well, I've always thought I'd make a rather dashing hero."

Carmella arched an eyebrow, her smile teasing. "Dashing, perhaps. But you'd have to behave yourself, Sir. No gallivanting off on secret missions without your wife's permission."

Robert feigned a serious expression. "A daunting challenge, indeed. But for you, my lady, I would undertake any feat."

They both laughed, the tension of the past slipping away in the light of their shared joy. Carmella's laughter softened into a smile as she studied him. "You've changed, Robert," she said quietly, her eyes warm. "You're... happier."

He nodded, his gaze holding hers. "I have you to thank for that," he replied. "You've given me a reason to believe in myself again, to see a future worth fighting for."

Her smile was soft and full of love. "And I'll keep believing in you, Robert. Whatever comes, we'll face it together."

He pulled her into his arms, holding her close as they stood in the warmth of their kitchen, surrounded by the love they had built together. For the first time in years, Robert felt a sense of contentment settle deep in his bones—a feeling that this, right here, was exactly where he was meant to be.

After a few moments, Carmella pulled back slightly, her eyes dancing with mischief once more. "But if you do decide to write back to North," she said, "make sure to let him know that I have no intention of sharing you with the Crown again."

Robert chuckled, his heart light. "I'll be sure to mention that." He took the letter from her hands, folding it carefully before setting it aside. "Besides, I think I've had quite enough of secret missions and hidden dangers for one lifetime."

She smiled, leaning up to press a soft kiss to his lips. "Good," she whispered. "Because I much prefer having you here with me."

Robert returned her kiss, his heart swelling with love. "And here is where I plan to stay," he promised. "For as long as you'll have me."

Carmella laughed, her eyes sparkling with happiness. "Oh, I think that can be arranged."

They shared a quiet moment together, basking in the simple joy of their newfound peace. Outside, the sun continued its climb into the sky, bathing the world in its warm, golden light. The future stretched out before them, bright and full of promise, and for the first time in his life, Robert felt truly at home.

As the morning sun streamed through the windows, casting dappled patterns on the floor, Robert took a deep breath, savouring the moment. He had found his place, his purpose, and most importantly, his heart. Here, in this quiet corner of Sussex, he had everything he needed.

His past might have been marked by hardship and regret, but his future was one of hope, filled with love and new beginnings. He had come a long way from the boy who had fled his home in disgrace, and he knew that whatever challenges lay ahead, he would face them with the strength of the woman he loved by his side.

Robert looked down at Carmella, her head resting against his shoulder, and felt a deep, abiding sense of gratitude. For the first time in his life, he felt truly whole.

From Nicole Clarkston

T HANK YOU FOR INDULGING with me and spending a little time with this sweet couple.

I hope you've had a delightful adventure! I would love it if you would share this family with your friends. As with all my books, I have enabled lending to make it easier to share. If you leave a review for *The Debutante and the Spy* on <u>Amazon</u>, <u>Goodreads</u>, <u>BookBub</u> or your own blog, I would love to read it! Email me the link at **<u>Author@NicoleClarksto</u> <u>n.com</u>**

And if you're hungry for more, including a gift ebook of *<u>The Ruin of Lord Aston's Daughter</u>*, stay up to date on upcoming releases and sales by <u>joining my newsletter:</u> https://subscribepage.io/V5dPFd

Keep reading for a sneak peek at *The Shepherdess and the Soldier!*

About Nicole

NICOLE CLARKSTON IS A book lover who fell in love with Jane Austen well into adult life. She has been obsessed ever since! She lives with her husband and three children in Oregon.

Nicole also writes flirty, satisfying novellas under the name Alix James.

Sign up for Nicole's Newsletter for a free gift and release news, or follow her blog at www.NicoleClarkston.com

You can also follow her at or the Austen Variations Newsletter.

www.ingramcontent.com/pod-product-compliance
Lightning Source LLC
Chambersburg PA
CBHW032211170626
46808CB00006B/2425